The Dyer Island Boys

by Jeffrey Veatch

Cover and interior design
by Vinnie Corbo

Volossal
Publishing

Published by Volossal Publishing
www.volossal.com

Copyright © 2022
ISBN 979-8-9850796-8-5

Table of Contents

Dedicated to my wife Marina,
daughter Elena, and late son Justin.

And to the rudderless teens and all those rooting
for them to find their compass.

Chapter One
The Lesson

It's low tide on a pristine August day at a rustic teen boys' camp on Dyer Island, Maine, two miles off the coast. A work project on a new pier is teeming with life. There is a steady stream of adolescent boys covered in mud and seaweed carrying heavy rocks from a grounded barge. The boys have formed a relay to hand the large rocks from one to another up to the top of a framework of logs that has been fastened together with steel rebar rods to form a square foundation for a new pier. Each rock is dropped into the cage to provide the weight necessary to keep the logs in place during the ebb and flow of the Maine tides. There is not an adult in sight and these boys seem to be enjoying the hard work, smiling and engaging in trash talk.

There is one exception. Fifteen-year-old Johnny Miller sits defiantly on a stack of pressure treated planking that will be used to construct the deck at the top of the pier. Johnny is small for his age, has a bad attitude, and is not fitting in. The very reason he is at this camp was discussed behind his back three months earlier by his mother, Carol, and New York City psychiatrist Dr. Peter Gallagher.

"I'm sorry Mrs. Miller. I can't help Johnny if he isn't present."

"But I'm afraid that's impossible under the circumstances," she replies.

"Tell me about those circumstances then," asks Dr. Gallagher.

"Johnny refuses to speak with anyone about his issues, even to the point of becoming violent," pleads Carol. "He has rebelled against everything. He's failed at school, can't keep friends, and he won't do anything responsible."

"What does he do?" asks Dr. Gallagher.

"In the year since his father's death," she explains while wringing her hands, "he has broken things, quit all sports, and sabotaged all new relationships I have developed with other men. He has no interests in anything but television and video games. I've tried counseling, rewarding, bribing, and everything."

Dr. Gallagher pauses to consider before scribbling on his notepad. He rips out a page and hands it to Carol.

"What is this?" she asks.

"It's a prescription for Xanax. It'll calm you down."

Dr. Gallagher turns to his notepad once more, pausing a moment before starting a fresh page.

"Johnny is not necessarily unique in his situation," he says. "I have a doctor friend, highly respected in medicine and in his community, who runs a summer camp for teens experiencing problems much like Johnny's. I'm certain if you give him a call, he will be willing to help."

At camp, Johnny continues to sit it out as other boys do the work. Fresh on his mind is what happened just two days earlier, when he decided to sneak into a cabin occupied by other boys while they were at the mess hall eating dinner.

Johnny was in the cabin going through some other boys' things. He found a box—a care package from home—and pulled out some new socks stuffing them into his back pocket. In a backpack beside one of the beds, Johnny picked up some folding money stuffing it into the same pocket. Sensing the boys were returning, he made a speedy exit when he was discovered by cabinmates Sean and TJ.

"Hey Johnny, what were you doing in our cabin?" asked Sean.

Johnny looked away in shame to avoid eye contact.

"What's that sticking out of your back pocket?" asked TJ.

"Those are my new socks," declared Sean who pulled them

out of Johnny's pocket. At the same time, the bills also tumbled onto the ground.

With that humiliation still in his head, Johnny ignores the work at the pier site. His mind strays to better times with his father whom he misses so dearly. His home life suffered when his father died a year ago and he now considers himself abandoned. He again longs for those days when his dad would take him fishing or canoeing— activities his mother has no interest in. His pleasant thoughts are now interrupted by Mark, a senior camp counselor who speaks with a strong Boston accent.

"Johnny, if you keep refusing to be a part of the work, nobody's gonna be your friend."

"I can do whatever the hell I want," replies Johnny.

"Yes," says Mark, "but you'll never be accepted and you're lookin' for a one-way ticket home."

"Fine by me," says Johnny.

"I've come because Wick wants to see you," adds Mark firmly as he ignores Johnny's response and points to a high point up the path where Wick's cabin is located.

Johnny grudgingly gets up and follows Mark on the path and up a hill toward Wick's Point, a high spot on the island. They arrive at an isolated cabin with a front deck that affords a grand view of the coastal water below. Mark knocks on the door and the two are greeted by Dr. Walter Wickson, a soft-spoken man of about eighty with white hair. Wick, as he is called by most, is a retired medical doctor who had been chairman of the surgical department at a major New York hospital. His wife, Dr. Anne Wickson, in her mid-seventies, a prominent retired pulmonologist, is with him.

"Dr. Wick," says Mark, "I have brought Johnny."

"Oh Johnny, I'm glad you came! Anne and I would like you to meet someone. But I'm afraid he is running a bit late. Please come in."

Johnny goes in while Mark waits outside.

"Mark, we'll be a little while. Johnny will rejoin his group when we're finished."

Mark heads back down the path and passes Harry Thompson, a distinguished looking black man of about sixty-five, who is heading up the hill, walking with a limp and aided by a cane. As they pass, Harry waves at Mark and speaks with a strong baritone voice. "You boys are doing some great work!"

"Thanks," replies Mark, "you know the motto."

"I surely do," says Harry.

When he arrives at Wick's cabin, Harry gives three loud knocks and enters without waiting. Inside, Wick is seated with Johnny and Anne drinking tea in the sparsely furnished living room. Wick gets up to greet Harry.

"It's really swell you could come out," says Wick, as he gives Harry a hug.

"I'd like you to meet Johnny Miller, one of our camp boys."

While Johnny does not get up, Harry offers a handshake.

"Johnny, this is Dr. Harold Thompson."

"Hello," Johnny responds shyly.

"Johnny is at Camp Dyer for the first time," explains Wick, "and I'm afraid he hasn't yet had a chance to fully appreciate what we're doing here."

"I can certainly understand," replies Harry turning to Johnny. "This island and this camp are very special to me. Maybe we can take a walk and I can point out some of that history."

Wick and Johnny get up while Anne decides to stay at the cabin.

"I'll pass on the walk while I catch up on my reading," offers Anne.

"Very well," says Wick as he, Johnny, and Harry head out. As they emerge, Wick and Harry slowly amble down the steps onto a path through the woods. Johnny follows along patiently, cutting his normal strides in half to keep from getting ahead. Faced with the prospect of having to explain his bad attitude, Johnny walks with trepidation. Johnny wasn't always like this. In school he was always taught to win whether it be grades or simply games of wit. No one ever spoke of losing. When Johnny's dad was battling cancer everyone said he was such a great fighter. When his dad lost that battle, Johnny was beaten too. His world was shattered. And then, when he and his mom moved to a new house and he started in a new school he was bullied for his size. On the path as they continue walking, Johnny is expecting to be reminded of his failures and told he will be sent home. But the reprimands don't come.

"I think I understand your feelings about going your own way," says Harry. "You're not much different from the way I was at your age. But there is one big difference."

"What's that?" asks Johnny.

"Well, for starters," offers Harry, "you have it much better than I did."

The three are passing an open space with a building that is much different from other island construction. It is made of granite stones and has large glass and stained glass windows that look out over the water. Harry moves off the path and gingerly over to the building, while Wick and Johnny stop. Harry runs his hands over the stone foundation and then examines the oversized front doors that have been artfully crafted from oak. As he continues to examine details at close range, Johnny looks at Wick in a puzzled way.

"The memorial building means a lot to him," explains Wick.

As Harry rejoins them, his face glowing with pride, they resume walking down the path.

"This island and this camp changed my life Johnny, but the story goes back even farther than that. This island wasn't meant to be what it is today. Dr. Wickson can tell you volumes about what happened even before they introduced me to this place."

"Well, Johnny," says Wick as they continue down the island path with Harry, "I was a young doctor in 1946 just beginning my career in New York. I worked as a resident at Roosevelt Hospital. That means I was a doctor but I needed practical training in treating patients. I was helping another resident, six years my senior, who had just come back home from World War II after it ended. Meredith Jones, like me, was studying to become a surgeon. We became close friends and even though he was technically my supervisor, I worked with him to update his medical skills and knowledge. I simply called him Doc and he called me Wick. We had big plans to save the world but no idea someday we would end up with this summer camp."

Chapter Two
The Beginnings

1946

Wick and Doc are both laughing as they approach an inner-city basketball court on the west side of Manhattan, dribbling a basketball and passing it while Doc smokes a cigarette. In a neighborhood where it's not uncommon to see boys fight over a pair of tattered shoes, Wick and Doc stand out in their white lab coats.

"Doctor Meredith Jones, resident extraordinaire," Wick taunts as he passes the ball.

"Doctor Walter Wickson, distinguished surgeon in training," Doc mocks right back. "Are you up to the art of throwing a ball through a hoop?" he asks as he dribbles and passes the ball back.

"I taught you everything you forgot while serving as an Army surgeon," quips Wick.

"That you did," admits Doc. "It's hard to mix good medicine and war."

The two young doctors locate their little brothers sitting on a nearby bench.

"Hello boys," calls Wick. "Are you ready to be challenged?"

"Bring it on," responds Julio, a slender eleven-year-old wearing a dirty t-shirt and ratty sneakers.

"If we win, can we keep the basketball?" asks his friend Jamie, who is fourteen, tall, and dressed similarly but sporting new sneakers.

"It's a deal," replies Doc who now joins Wick in removing his lab coat.

Wick and Doc are not exactly dressed for the part with the leather shoes and regular pants they had worn during their latest hospital rounds. Wick throws the ball to Julio who starts the half-court game by throwing it to Jamie who is challenged by Doc. Jamie dribbles around both men as he drives in for an easy layup.

"Did I tell you I'm a point guard on the PS 111 middle school team?" he boasts.

Wick passes to Doc who returns the ball back after a few awkward dribbles. Wick's attempt at a fifteen-footer bounces off the rim as Jamie grabs the rebound. He feeds the ball to Julio for a shot that rolls around the rim and in. And so it goes over the next twenty minutes as Wick calls time with a score of twenty to four.

"Okay, little brothers. You're the champs for today," declares Wick.

"And that means you get to keep the ball," says Doc as he tosses it to Jamie.

"Yeah, we work the court," exclaims Julio.

"Be sure you bring it back when we meet next week," adds Wick.

As the doctors put their lab coats back on Julio and Jamie continue to dribble and shoot baskets.

Heading back towards the hospital, Doc lights another cigarette and draws a comment from a petite twenties-something woman with rather stunning eyes who is sitting on a park bench with a book on her lap. She is Dr. Anne Dobson, a senior resident at nearby Bellevue Hospital, wearing an attractive black dress under her white lab coat.

"You could set a better example," she says, looking at Doc.

"I beg your pardon?" says Doc.

"The cigarette," she scolds. "You are obviously a doctor and you are obviously influencing these young boys."

Wick smiles and stays out of the conversation, leaving Doc to finesse the moment on his own.

"You're right, ma'am," Doc admits. "It's a bad habit from the war."

He bows slightly but keeps his cigarette. As he and Wick resume walking, Wick confides that Anne has gotten his attention.

"If she comes back every day, I'll spend even more time on the court," Wick says with a smile and a chuckle.

As the two young doctors pass a street vendor, a teenage boy is delivering a package in a plain brown wrapper.

Harry Thompson, a slim fifteen-year-old black boy dressed in modest and well-worn clothes, goes about his rounds selling smuggled contraband cigarettes to skirt the state tobacco tax. It's not a scheme he ever pictured himself getting wrapped up in, but he accepts it as his only option to make fifty cents on every delivery. His father was killed in the war and his mother, now a widow, struggles to make ends meet.

"Here are the smokes from South Carolina," Harry tells the man with the street cart as he hands him the package.

"Keep it quiet," the man sternly reprimands. "You want me arrested?"

"I'm supposed to collect six dollars and fifty cents," replies Harry.

"What?" the vendor protests.

"Between you and me, I've already paid for these," the man says in a stern whisper. "Can't help it if you got robbed. Tell your boss that or I'll report you to the cops."

Harry struggles to grab the package back but the man with the cart wins the battle. Harry knows he needs to be tough to survive in his environment but tough is not who he really is. With incidents like this, his self-esteem is suffering. Harry leaves empty handed except for a small, well-worn paper bag in one of his back pockets. In his mind, he is beating himself up for giving up too easily. Rather than fight, he'd rather just walk and think.

What is my life about? Where am I heading?

Harry arrives at a half abandoned walk-up apartment building in a neighborhood that displays the signs that many others have given up too. He pulls the crumpled paper bag out of his back pocket. Questionable characters loiter by the front stoop as Harry enters and walks up the stairs.

"Hey, Harry. What's up?" The man who speaks is drinking out of a bottle in a paper bag.

Harry ignores him, hastens up the steps to the third floor, and knocks on the door.

"Who's there?" asks a woman on the inside behind the closed door.

"It's Harry. Can I see Roseanne?"

"I'm not decent," she replies through the door which remains shut, "and Roseanne's having one of her attacks."

Harry is disappointed and bangs his fist against the door frame but gives up for the time being as he smells the fumes of cigarette smoke leaking out from the apartment.

"I'll come back later," Harry shouts through the closed door.

He worries about Roseanne, a slight and pale fourteen-year-old half-sister he has never spoken about with his mom because she thinks he doesn't know about her. He knows Roseanne's foster parents don't let her go out much and she suffers breathing problems in the confines of their apartment. When his dad told him about Roseanne before he left for the war, Harry promised to keep it to himself but made it a point to keep tabs on her. He knew where she lived and that the building had no super in charge of things. So, he brought his pigeon loft to the roof of the building. He made it a point to check on Roseanne as a matter of routine. And then one day they went for a walk together up past Columbus Circle and into Central Park.

"I love the park," says Harry.

"I do too," replies Roseanne, "the air is so clean and it's like being in another world. And I can actually breathe."

"When I come by your foster mother never wants to let me see you. Why is that?" Harry asks.

"They don't like it when I leave," says Roseanne. "It's like they think I'm gonna run away."

"Why don't you?" asks Harry. "I know Dad would rather see you living with us."

"He was so kind to me," admits Roseanne. "He used to always carry me on his shoulders and I was never afraid of falling." She pauses in thought. "No one ever cared for me like he did. And Mom was never there. She was there, but didn't seem to be caring. It really hurt when we lost Dad."

"Yeah," says Harry. "I had the same feelings about Dad." Harry pauses as though he is afraid to ask Roseanne the next question. "What actually happened to your mom?"

"I can't really say what happened," says Roseanne. "She got caught up with some dope ring in the neighborhood. And then one day the police came to our door. She was in the middle of a dispute that turned violent. I can't…" Roseanne is tearing up. "I can't understand why. I can't…"

"That's okay," says Harry. "I understand."

They're now walking in a part of the park with hundreds of yellow flowers on each side of the woodchip path.

"I wish life was better for us," says Harry. "I wish it was a place where flowers bloom unbound by space or time. Free of the bleak and bland, our spirits never low."

"That's beautiful," says Roseanne. "Is that from a poem?"

"I don't know," says Harry. "It just came into my head. And it seems to fit."

Ever since that walk, Harry and Roseanne have considered themselves brother and sister even though their family lives are detached. Harry gets frustrated when he comes by Roseanne's and her foster mom won't let him in to see her.

Instead of leaving Roseanne's building, Harry now goes on up the steps to the top of the 8th floor and opens a door to the roof of the building. This is his refuge from the tough world below where he keeps pigeons. He goes over to a pigeon loft where there are about a dozen birds, reaches in to pull one out, and kisses it. Harry then whistles, gives the bird a slight heave, and the pigeon flies high into the air, circling around the rooftops of nearby buildings. Harry imagines himself in flight over the world below where the neighborhood is not always so kind. He's seen boys his age shaken down by neighborhood gangs, some of them threatened with knives. There are good people all around, of course, but his fear of encountering the wrong ones is always with him.

Harry whistles again and the pigeon he took out flies back down right onto the porch of the loft.

"Good baby," says Harry affectionately. "You are my Flying Dutchman."

Harry cradles and kisses his "Dutchman" and places seeds from the bag he was carrying into the loft where the bird follows. Pigeon keeping is pretty common on rooftops in this neighborhood, but Harry is convinced he has one of the best birds to ever fly.

Harry then moves over to a corner interior of the wall on the roof where there are a few loose bricks. He removes one of them and pulls out a can containing some coins and folding money. He counts it and puts it back. It reminds him of times his dad bought him things like balls and other toys. Now he's on his own for things like that. His thoughts drift back in time to when he was ten, playing ball with his dad in Central Park. He daydreams about having been part of a real family before the streets around his west side neighborhood of Hell's Kitchen took over his life.

Across town on the east side of Manhattan, Anne Dobson is on her way to an upper floor of Bellevue Hospital. She is dressed smartly in a business suit and pumps. In the elevator, she coughs a couple of times and clears her throat before she arrives at the floor containing the offices of Dr. Richard Simpson, a high-level hospital executive. She is cheerfully greeted in an outer office by Dr. Simpson's secretary.

"Hello, Dr. Dobson. Dr. Simpson is expecting you. You may go right in."

As Anne enters, she is taken by the stunning view north to Central Park and east to Long Island Sound, the fine woods in the furniture, and the bold, but tasteful colors. Dr. Simpson, a well-dressed man in his fifties, gets up from his desk and comes around to shake her hand.

"It's nice to meet you at long last," he says. "You have achieved quite a lot in your senior residency here. Have you thought about your next move?"

"Well," responds Anne, "I'm hoping Bellevue will have a place for me."

"That's good news," responds Dr. Simpson. "I'll get right to the point. Your research on COPD has been very impressive. We'd like to recommend you for a fellowship grant offered by the Trudeau Society."

Anne is pleasantly stunned by Dr. Simpson's response. She has always been an overachiever, graduating at the top of her class in medical school. She has long been on a mission to make a big difference in the world of pulmonology. The work is intuitive and immensely satisfying to her, but the journey has not been easy.

"That would be wonderful!" she responds, gleeful, as Dr. Simpson jumps on her favorable reaction to seal the deal.

"This fellowship could give you an opportunity to begin real case studies on emphysema patients. And that fits into our plans to open the first emphysema clinic in New York. What do you say?"

"What do I say?" responds Anne. "It's exactly what I'm hoping for!"

"Very well," says Dr. Simpson who is actually relieved that he didn't have to hard sell to his most promising prospect. "We'll start the process then."

Anne gets up to shake his hand. "Thank you so much, Dr. Simpson."

"We'll be getting some forms over to you," he replies. "And… congratulations once again!"

Anne floats out of the office with a broad smile. As she walks toward the elevator, she stifles a cough, then does cough rather forcefully into a handkerchief. She looks at the handkerchief and her smile turns into an expression of concern when she discovers it freshly spattered with blood.

Back across town in a drab apartment on the West Side near Roosevelt Hospital, a woman holds a photograph of an American serviceman next to a table lamp. Also on the table is an American flag folded in a frame with two purple hearts, a distinguished service cross, and a gold star affixed to it. Thelma Thompson, a stocky woman in her thirties, puts down the photograph and picks up a photo of Harry.

"Harry, why are you punishing me this way? Your father would be ashamed of us," she says tearfully to the picture.

Having lost her husband in the war just four years ago, Thelma struggles to make ends meet. She works at nearby Roosevelt Hospital disinfecting operating rooms on the night shift and her unusual hours make it difficult to spend quality time with Harry.

The knob on the apartment door rattles and then there is the sound of a loud bam on the door.

"Harry, is that you?"

Harry shouts from the other side of the door. "Why'd you lock the damn door? Let me in!"

As Thelma opens the door, Harry rushes in and looks around the apartment without paying attention to her, searching for something.

"Harry, it's late, and why don't you have your key? What are you looking for?"

Harry pulls something out of a drawer and puts it in his pocket. He says nothing as he rushes for the door.

"Where are you going at this hour?" Thelma pleads.

"I'm taking care of something," he barks.

As Harry slams the door behind him, Thelma falls to her knees in tears.

I'm not tough enough, Harry thinks as he walks down the street not knowing where he's going or why he's out there. Harry has grown tired of carrying the weight of a secret—that he and Roseanne share the same father. He knows he could confront his mother and put an end to the charade. But he's never known how to ask for help, and continues to quietly take matters into his own hands.

He wouldn't need to peddle cigarettes on the streets if Roseanne hadn't lost her mother in a gang fight. But that's the reality as Roseanne is now an orphan in the eyes of the state.

"I've got to rescue her. I've got to rescue her," Harry repeats to himself. *If only I can get enough money to send her to a doctor,* Harry thinks, *maybe Mom will make an effort to bring us together.*

Harry hears more voices from his darker angels as he continues to wander the streets.

Wick walks home after his stint at Roosevelt Hospital. As he is turning a corner toward his apartment, Harry, who has pulled out a knife, confronts him.

"Give me your money," Harry demands, brandishing his weapon.

Wick is stunned by the threat but thinks he may be able to talk sense to his attacker.

"Take it easy young man," he pleads. "I'm a doctor and I can help you."

"You can only help me by giving me your wallet," shouts Harry as he continues to threaten with the knife.

Wick pulls out his wallet and Harry grabs it and runs. Minutes later, Wick is sitting at a desk cluttered with papers in his apartment. He has dialed the police on the telephone.

"Sergeant, I want to report a robbery," he says. "I'm a doctor at Roosevelt Hospital and I was accosted by a mugger a few minutes ago."

"Were you injured?" asks the desk sergeant who is taking down the information.

"No," Wick replies, "but he took my wallet and I'm pretty upset."

Wick remembers the time he was mugged when he was a student. The girl who was with him at the time put up a fight and she was hurt by the attacker.

"I'm actually quite fearful of muggers," admits Wick.

"You did the right thing by not putting up a fight," assures the sergeant. "Can you describe the attacker?"

"Yes," Wick responds. "He was a young Negro in his teens. He threatened me with his knife. How can a doctor feel safe? I hope you can find him."

"I'll report this information," says the sergeant, "but you'll have to come down to the 20th precinct. Can you do that in the morning?"

"Certainly, Sergeant," Wick responds, "Thank you."

On an empty street near 57th, Harry watches his back as he rushes away after spotting a patrol car. Harry's guilt has him in panic mode and has drawn the attention of the officers. As the patrol car pulls up beside him on the street, Harry stops.

"How old are you, young man?" asks one of the officers.

"I'm fifteen," says Harry nervously.

"It's nearly midnight," the officer says, "and we had a radio report that a man was accosted and robbed just three blocks away. Do you have a reason to be out at this hour?"

"No sir, I'm just walking," replies Harry.

Harry's conscience has already gotten the best of him as he knew the moment he ran with the wallet he couldn't possibly live the life of a mugger. He is relieved when the officer asks him to empty his pockets.

"I didn't mean to hurt anyone," says Harry who hands the officer Wick's wallet as well as the knife he had brought with him. "I've never done anything like this before. I need the money to help a friend go to a doctor."

"Well, son, the man you robbed *is* a doctor," says the officer. "I'm afraid you'll have to come with us."

He handcuffs Harry and leads him into the back seat of the patrol car.

The next morning, Wick quickly gets dressed and dashes over to the station where a policeman guides him to a workspace to fill out a report. The officer then places Wick's wallet on the desk.

"We found your wallet when we stopped a young man in the neighborhood late last night," says the officer. "Do you recall how much money was in it?"

"I think I had a five and two singles, seven dollars. I had some change in my pocket but he didn't get that."

The officer hands it to Wick.

"You're lucky. There's still seven dollars in it. And your driver's license and identification cards seem to be intact."

Wick examines it as the officer tells him about the young man they are holding.

"His name is Harry Thompson and he's fifteen. He's now in booking with his mother." The officer hands him a form to sign. "I'll need your signature on this complaint."

Wick is not paying attention to the paper, but repeats the name.

"Thompson. I know a Mrs. Thompson at the hospital. Is it possible for me to see her?

"I'm afraid that would violate police policy," he replies as Wick signs the form.

"We'll need you to appear before a judge to press charges," says the officer as he directs Wick back to the entrance. "You'll get a court date in the mail."

As Wick walks the hallway toward the entrance, he spots Thelma Thompson, recognizes her, and rushes over.

"Thelma! How are you doing? I'm here because I was robbed last night. Is Harry your son?"

"Doctor," Thelma replies as tears stream down her face. "I'm so sorry."

"I had no idea he was your son," Wick says, hoping to comfort her as he gives her a hug.

"I don't know what has gotten into Harry," Thelma confides. "Since his father died in the war, he's been harder and harder to deal with."

"I got everything back," says Wick. "Let me talk with the officer. I won't press charges and maybe I can get them dropped."

As Wick and Doc walk back from the basketball court after another informal game with their little brothers, Doc is asking about the incident with Harry.

"He turns out to be the son of one of the night cleaning ladies," says Wick. "Thelma Thompson scrubs down the operating rooms at night. She's a hard worker and a good person. Harry's father died in the war and I couldn't allow him to be sent to jail."

"Do you think he'll stay out of trouble?" Doc asks.

"We can only hope," replies Wick. "For a boy that age, the loss of a father during battle in the war has a big impact."

"I have great respect for the Negro men who fought along side of us," says Doc. "As a matter of fact, I owe a huge debt of gratitude to one who saved my life toward the end of the war."

"What happened?" asks Wick.

"I was in Burma treating a wounded GI in the jungle when a Japanese soldier was about to attack us. I didn't see him but the GI's comrade did and shot the Jap dead before he could pull off the shot. My savior was a tank gunner, a Negro, who was staying with his buddy after he was wounded."

"Doc, I never knew you were so close to combat," says an astonished Wick. "Were you able to save the soldier?"

"Yes," says Doc. "He was later taken to a field hospital where I heard he was doing fine."

"Were you able to thank his buddy?" asks Wick.

"I tried," replies Doc, "but found out he died in action just days later and the Army hasn't located the records with his name and exactly what happened."

In a West Side alley way, Harry lines up among a dozen or so boys behind a small truck where a man is unloading bundles of contraband cigarettes in plain brown paper packages like the one Harry delivered to the street vendor. They are being distributed to those in line as names are checked off a list.

Harry is fortunate that Wick dropped the robbery charges against him and since it was a first offense, he was let off the hook. The memory of what he did that night burns in his heart and he never wants to experience that again.

Harry gets to the front of the line and gives his name.

"I'm Harry Thompson and I can't pay what I owe because I was robbed by the man who wanted to buy 'em."

"You owe us six dollars," says the man in the back of the truck. "And you ain't gettin' any more 'till you pay up."

"But I was robbed," argues Harry.

"Tell it to the guy up front," he says as he points behind him.

Harry walks up to the cab and steps up to the window. A sleezy-looking man in his thirties sits on the passenger side counting money.

"You Harry?" he asks. "You ain't gettin' any more 'till you pay up."

"But I was robbed," pleads Harry. "I plan to pay you back by selling more."

The man in the cab points to the end of the alley way.

"Meet me in my office," he says.

The man puts the money away, gets out of the truck, and motions for Harry to walk with him deeper into the dead-end alley. He then pulls out a switchblade knife.

"See this?" he says as he waves it back and forth. "This is what you use to keep people from robbing you."

He puts the knife back in his pocket and then surprises Harry with a punch in the stomach. It sends Harry to the ground.

"And that's what'll happen if you come around here again without the money."

The man leaves Harry there and walks back to the truck.

Harry is okay, but rethinking whether this is the best way to get money to help Roseanne. In his neighborhood, jobs are scarce as the war effort hasn't benefited Black New Yorkers as much as it did others, especially for teens like him. He's tried the local stores and shops, which are reluctant to have a shabbily dressed kid like him around. Unlike the suburbs, there are no lawns to mow or shrubs to trim in his neighborhood. Harry thought about becoming a delivery boy but he has no bicycle and can't afford one anyway. He also tried the bowling alley where pins have to be set by hand but ended up terrified that he could be hurt by flying pins and errant balls like one boy he heard about. Harry wants to confront his mother about Roseanne but he thinks if he makes his own money to help her, his mother will have no excuse but to do what she can to bring Roseanne into the family.

Wick and Doc, dressed in business suits, enter a large meeting room just off the lobby of a fancy Midtown hotel. A sign at the entrance reads "Welcome New York Thoracic Society." They pass an open bar with guests smoking cigarettes. Doc lights one up for himself. Wick has talked Doc into coming tonight because he thinks it will be wise to connect with physicians in the various fields of medicine and perhaps make some connections.

"It's about who you know," reminds Wick. "A good time to stop and smell the roses," he adds.

Their conversation is abruptly interrupted as an attractive yet nervous young woman rushing through the crowd bumps into Wick and drops some papers on the carpet. As Wick helps her retrieve them he realizes it's the woman they encountered at the basketball court. Their eyes lock briefly before she rushes off, prompting a comment from Doc.

"Smell the roses?" he asks.

"I'll never forget those eyes. Definitely a rose," replies Wick as he smiles.

Wick and Doc wind their way through the crowd. As they enter a banquet hall Wick spots Anne heading up to the front where she sits with a group of speakers on the dais. Wick finds a table as close to the front as possible and Doc joins him there. From a speakers list in the program Wick learns her name and her background.

"She's a pulmonary resident," says Wick.

"Who is the she you are referring to?" asks Doc, clueless about Wick's line of thinking.

"Her name is Anne Dobson," says Wick. "She's the one who dressed you down at the basketball court."

"Oh yes," realizes Doc. "I remember her. This could be interesting," he muses as he lights another cigarette.

Those in the audience are professionals and some are taking notes as they hear from one pulmonologist after another. Finally, Anne is introduced by the master of ceremonies.

"It is finally my pleasure to introduce a recent graduate of Columbia's College of Physicians and Surgeons," he announces. "Her work in chronic obstructive pulmonary disease is turning a few heads.

She has recently been named the recipient of a Trudeau Fellowship at Bellevue Hospital. Please join me in welcoming Dr. Anne Dobson."

Anne is greeted with polite applause and begins her speech.

"I would like to thank Dr. Richard Simpson and colleagues at Roosevelt for inviting me tonight."

As she gets into her talk, most of the audience loses interest, but Wick finds himself captivated by how passionately she speaks about the dangers of cigarette smoke. Some of the audience has left before she concludes her talk.

"And so while the data we've examined on these emphysema cases is not yet conclusive," she pauses with a slight cough, "I think it would be fair to say that rooms like this one filled with smoke from cigarettes could not be considered a healthy environment for either young children or patients in distress with chronic pulmonary issues. Thank you."

The applause for Anne is polite but sparse except for the enthusiastic one-man standing ovation coming from Wick, who then moves through the departing crowd up to the dais to say hello.

"I really appreciate what you had to say, Dr. Dobson," praises Wick as he shakes Anne's hand. "It's not the easiest topic to present to a crowd like this."

"Thank you. I don't think it went over as well as I had hoped, but it's a start," Anne admits.

"Passion is what you have," assures Wick. "It's totally lacking in many who take on this profession. I'm Walter Wickson, a surgical intern at Roosevelt."

"Pleased to meet you," Anne replies.

"Friends just call me Wick. Did I see you last week reading near the basketball courts? I'm afraid my friend Doc didn't make the best impression."

"That was you with him," Anne realizes. "Offer my apologies for my frankness. Smoking is a terrible habit but especially when it comes to influencing young people."

"But you were spot on!" Wick acknowledges while overdramatizing his praise with hand gestures. "Doc served in the Army in the war and got closer to the actual fighting than others. It's a real stress trigger."

Wick pauses as he tries to find an angle to see Anne again.

"Will I see you in the park?" asks Wick.

"Depends," says Anne with a coy smile.

Wick nervously falters on a clever followup.

"Again, my congratulations on your work," says Wick shyly, not really wanting to end the conversation but also aware others are waiting to say hello.

As Wick rejoins Doc, he regrets not having gotten her telephone number.

"I see you are taking a stronger interest in thoracic medicine," says Doc with a touch of sarcasm.

"She's a fine lady," replies Wick, "a very fine lady."

Still on the dais, Anne is wrapping up her conversations and looks around to see if Wick is still there.

Chapter Three
The Island Beckons

It's Sunday morning. Wick is in his apartment reading The New York Times real estate section and comes across an ad that makes him mutter to himself. "How about that?"

A knock on the door announces Doc's arrival for their Sunday brunch plans.

"Let's try Dino's on 57th," says Doc. "I hear their Sunday brunch is really special."

"Sounds good to me," replies Wick, "but look at this."

Wick shows Doc the ad and Doc reads it out loud.

"One thousand acre island, two miles off the coast of Maine offered for sale by The Seaboard Paper Company. Pulpwood supply has been cut. Will sell for $1,500."

"Wouldn't it be swell if we could buy this for summer adventure?" wonders Wick. "It's undeveloped and we could blow off steam and return to our scouting roots."

Wick and Doc have a common bond through the things they did in scouting as young teens. Wick was an Eagle Scout and Doc had been close to achieving that honor. Wick fondly recalls sharing with Doc the joys he experienced while doing medical research on

Forbes Island, British Columbia studying the anatomy of deer antlers, experiencing the wild in a natural setting with no telephones and no interruptions. They hit it off immediately when they first met as Doc was applying for a residency at Roosevelt Hospital.

Doc had just finished a tour of duty in WWII and Wick was already established in his surgical residency. They often talked about the adventures they had as scouts in the wild while navigating city life.

"Don't we have enough to handle in this city jungle?" reasons Doc. "We aren't even established yet."

"But I think it's a great opportunity for the future," replies Wick. "Who knows exactly where we're headed? But we know one thing for certain. We both enjoy adventure in the wild. I'll bet the payments would be modest. I'm going to check it out."

Anne waits nervously in an exam room in the office of Dr. Albert Shaw, a pulmonologist specializing in tuberculosis at Bellevue Hospital. Dr. Shaw enters and places x-ray charts on his display screen mounted on the wall.

"Anne, I'm afraid your suspicions were well founded. Your x-rays confirm it. But the good news is you caught it early."

Anne looks worried. "The bad news is there is no cure for tuberculosis," she counters.

"But at this early stage," he responds, "I'm confident you will respond very well to the treatment protocol. And there is a new drug."

"Streptomycin from Rutgers," Anne fires back.

"Very experimental," he says, "and we're not at that stage where you're struggling to clear your lungs. You're very lucky you are knowledgeable enough to recognize that fever, chills, ongoing coughing and night sweats were the early signs something serious was going on."

"But not careful enough to prevent the infection in the first place," Anne admits.

"It's impossible for a doctor with daily exposure to patients to be completely safe," says Dr. Shaw, trying to ease Anne's concern.

Anne nods in agreement as tears begin to stream down her face. She clutches her hands together in an attempt to comfort herself but her eyes give away her deep inner disappointment and anxiety.

"I'm admitting you to the isolation ward on strict bed rest where we can carefully monitor your situation," orders Dr. Shaw.

Anne has the look of a great athlete experiencing the agony of defeat.

"I'm afraid I'm a bit out of my element," she admits meekly. "I'm used to taking bold steps and helping patients find cures. Now, I'm supposed to lay on my back and do nothing for perhaps eight or even sixteen months."

"But you won't be alone. And you might be able to continue some of your work here at Bellevue," offers the doctor.

Anne is silent as she tries to wrap her mind around what's happening. She's worked so hard for this opportunity and failure at this point for her is unthinkable.

"Is there anyone you have been in close contact with who we need to reach?" Dr. Shaw asks.

At Wick's apartment, Wick and Doc peer at a map of Maine. "I spent several summers exploring Acadia National Park," Wick says as he points to the location. "Dyer Island is just a little farther north off DownEast Maine. The land was originally claimed by the French and extends up into the Canadian Provinces. It's one of the most beautiful rocky coastal areas I've ever seen."

"I agree," says Doc as he looks through a magnifying glass. "The island is just a speck on the map but really close to the coastal town of Milbridge." He uses a ruler to measure the distance on the map. "According to this map it's about two miles. I'll bet we could actually row a boat from there to Dyer. But we dare not miss it, or we'd be on our way to Nova Scotia and the Bay of Fundy."

The Bay of Fundy is one of the Seven Wonders of North America. It has the highest tides on earth, the rarest whales in the world, semi-precious minerals, and some of the most treacherous waters along the East Coast.

"I've already called the Bank of New York," says Wick who is more convinced the purchase would be a wise investment. "The loan officer I spoke with was very encouraging. He said the government is eager to help veterans with loan guarantees. I'm expecting to hear back from him any time."

The telephone rings and Wick answers.

"Hello?"

"This is Marc Bravely from the Bank of New York. I'm afraid obtaining a loan for the island purchase will require a down payment of thirty percent and, of course, the island itself would become collateral for the bank."

"I understand," replies Wick. "We'll try to come up with it."

"Let me know," replies Mr. Bravely, "and we can then initiate a title search."

"Thank you, Mr. Bravely. I hope to be in touch soon." Wick hangs up.

"That was Mr. Bravely from the bank," says Wick as he calculates the numbers. "We can't get a loan without a down payment of $450 up front."

That was more money than they had, even if they combined assets from both their checking accounts. Wick is not discouraged as he delves deeper into the possibilities.

"I can't help thinking of people like Harry and Thelma who have no means for a change in scenery," offers Wick. "Just think about the enormity of owning an island as a getaway spot, not only for us but one we could share with others."

The telephone rings again and Wick answers.

"Hello? Thelma! I was just thinking about you and Harry."

"I'm afraid Harry's run away," she confides as she begins to sob. "I'm so sorry to bother you but I have no one else to ask for help."

"Don't apologize," says Wick. "I told you to call me any time. Hold on just one moment."

Wick puts the telephone down and whispers to Doc.

"Harry's mom says he's run away. She's only four blocks away. I think I'd better go over there. Want to join me?"

"Sure," says Doc.

Wick is back on the phone with Thelma. "I have a colleague with me who also is a Big Brother. Can we stop by your apartment?"

"I'm so sorry to trouble you, but I'm not sure what to do," Thelma says.

"Just stay put and we'll be over in a few minutes," assures Wick.

Thelma grew up in Puerto Rico with indigenous Tainos whose ancestors date back to the beginning of island life. She was drawn to New York City when she was nineteen, knowing that as a United States citizen she could take advantage of greater opportunities. Unfortunately, she had to overcome numerous hurdles including discrimination and lack of technical skills. While living with relatives in East Harlem she held numerous odd jobs and had hoped to be schooled in nursing. Then she met Walter Thompson, her husband and Harry's father, who was a sewing machine operator in the New York City garment industry. They caught each other's eyes at a dance club in Harlem in 1929 and quickly fell in love. They were married in 1930. When Thelma gave birth to Harry, her dreams of becoming a nurse faded. Walter worked long, hard hours at his job and decided to join the U.S. Army before World War II, hoping the military training would provide him new skills for a better job at home. With his recent death in the battlefield, Thelma continued to struggle with meager GI benefits and her low paying job at Roosevelt Hospital.

When Wick and Doc arrive at her apartment, Thelma is nearly inconsolable.

"I thought Harry was better. But when I got home from the overnight shift, he wasn't here. And he didn't come home for dinner. And some of his things are gone. I'm really concerned he's gotten involved with some of the gang members who have claimed our neighborhood."

"What gang is that?" asks Wick.

"The Dragons," replies Thelma. "They were involved in a street fight just two blocks away and Harry says he's been trying to steer clear."

"Has Harry been confronted directly?" asks Wick.

"Well yes," says Thelma, "and he's been asked to join the Dragons but he wants no part of it."

"Don't worry," assures Wick. "We'll try to help you find Harry."

"Is there someone you think he might be staying with?" asks Doc.

"There's Tommy who works at the corner grocery. And then there's Arthur, a parking lot attendant after school. But I don't know their families or where they live. They hang out at the bowling alley on 57th but when I went there I didn't see them."

"Do you have a picture of Harry we can borrow?" asks Wick.

"Yes."

While she searches her purse, Doc picks up the picture of her late husband on the table and looks at the medals on the folded flag.

"I served in the same theater," says Doc. "Your husband was a real hero. So sorry, ma'am."

Thelma hands a picture to Wick. "This is from last year," she says.

Wick and Doc leave Thelma's as the sun is setting. It's after dark as Wick and Doc depart from the 57th Street bowling alley without having located Harry.

Wick knows that Doc is scheduled for an early shift at the hospital the next day. "It's getting late, Doc, and you're on call early. Why don't you go home and I'll continue to look around for a while longer?"

"Be careful," says Doc. "I'll check with you in the morning."

Minutes later, Wick arrives at the Columbus Avenue subway station entrance on 59th Street. He hurries down the steps and approaches a turnstile leading to one of the train platforms. A panhandler wearing a U.S. Army cap displays a sign: "Help a homeless war vet." Wick drops a few coins into his cup and shows the man the picture of Harry. "Have you seen this boy?"

The man shakes his head, and Wick heads back up the steps empty handed. Meanwhile, in a dark nearby corner Wick missed, Harry crouches down with a small bag of his belongings. After a few minutes Harry, who is alone, goes back up the steps to the street and walks over to a grocery store near his apartment building. He sees stacks of empty soda bottles in a caged area in the back of the store and thinks he could make money by gathering the bottles for deposit refunds.

Harry is not a joiner. He's an introvert and fears his quiet ways make him weaker and less able to be a success at something. He'd rather think things out on his own. He's stymied by his bleak job prospects and is always thinking about angles. He's a natural saver. A nickel and dime here and there add up to dollars in the long run. That's why he keeps his can of money in its hiding place.

The problem at hand now for Harry is how will he gather up enough of those bottles in the cage and cash them in. He's not thinking about them as someone else's property. He spots an empty case at the base of the cage and reasons he could fill that up and nobody would miss a few bottles anyway. He looks around and then goes for the latch on the door. It's not locked, so he goes in and fills the case with bottles. But his plan goes awry when he sets off an alarm. A patrol car with two police officers arrives immediately and a bright light shines in his eyes.

"Don't move!" orders a police officer who approaches to get a better look.

"What's your name?" asks the other officer. "Do you have an ID and what are you doing on this property?"

Harry reaches into his back pocket and pulls out a dog tag which belonged to his father.

"My name is Harry Thompson. This was my dad's dog tag from the war. I thought these bottles were being thrown out."

"This store has been robbed a few times," says the first officer, "and you are trespassing on their property. I'm afraid you'll have to come with us."

Anne lies flat on her back in the Bellevue Hospital tuberculosis ward. There are flowers and cards on a side table. The Harmonicats hit song "Peg of My Heart" plays on the radio. In walks Dr. Simpson, the hospital administrator Anne met with before her diagnosis. He wears a surgical mask, but Anne recognizes him right away.

"Dr. Simpson. What a pleasant surprise!"

"I wanted to check on you. How is our star patient?" he asks.

"I'm as good as expected. I do hope you're being careful, the germs I mean."

"Anne, I've been in and out of these wards all my career. I'm afraid this room is the best we can do for you, but it is private."

"You've been so kind," says Anne. "And I'm sorry about what happened."

"Sorry? Don't be silly," he chides. "Becoming infected is a risk we all take. A fork in the road is not the end of the road unless you fail to make the right turn. You're making that turn. Have you seen your folks?"

"Yes, my parents were here this morning. I told them not to come by too often, but I think they're having a difficult time accepting the fact that I have TB."

"Anne," Dr. Shaw says as he clears his throat, "I want you to know the people at Trudeau know about your illness. The grant will still be yours, but work on the project will slow down until you're well enough to come onboard."

"Thank you! I don't know what to say."

"No words are necessary. One of the board members told me he thinks you'll be a better research fellow because of this experience."

"I hope so," replies Anne.

"We won't push you, but as long as your infection is in check, I'll be sending over some materials to review. That is, if you feel up to it," he adds.

"So far, I feel fine with hardly any fever."

"Good. If it stays that way, you are one of the lucky ones. Expect to be here a few months. And then we'll get you over to Trudeau in Saranac Lake."

Anne laughs nervously. "They give me a grant and now I'm their patient."

"Well, Anne, life is full of ironies."

Wick and Doc walk along Central Park West at lunch time.

"Mrs. Thompson must be pretty upset about Harry's arrest," says Doc.

"She's at her wit's end," says Wick. "But she also seems relieved he hadn't gotten involved with The Dragons. They're keeping Harry at Lavenburg Youth House until his case comes before a judge."

"Mayor O'Dwyer is trying to close that place," says Doc. "Any chance they'll free him in his mother's custody?"

"Not until he has a hearing," Wick replies. "A change in scenery probably won't hurt. Thelma says the only place Harry has ever known is his neighborhood. In fact, he's never been outside of the island of Manhattan."

That's sad," says Doc. "But I'm afraid the scenery at Lavenburg won't help Harry."

The Lavenburg Youth House was opened in 1928 as an all-girls' institution, but was turned into a home for troubled boys in the 1940s. It was rife with stories of corruption and bigotry when it came to dealing with racial minorities. It never was a true detention center nor a psychiatric hospital and fights among some of its more aggressive inmates were known to be commonplace. As an introvert, Harry might easily avoid being caught up in that violence.

As Wick and Doc continue to discuss Harry's plight, Doc makes a connection between Harry and the island they are considering buying off Maine.

"Learning to live with nature and without the noise of daily city life can do wonders for a teenage boy," reasons Doc.

He thinks back and tells Wick about a camping trip with his troop when he was eleven.

"We were in the foothills of the Berkshire Mountains as Boy Scouts," says Doc. "We were camping along a stream. It was a perfect site for a camp until the rain came. It rained so hard even the trenches we dug around the tent didn't prevent the floor from turning into mud. As we were looking for refuge our scout leader knew of an abandoned mansion nearby where we could set up camp. We found enough dry wood for a fire in the fireplace which thankfully was in working condition and swapped ghost stories all night long. We didn't sleep much, but in the morning I felt as rested as I'd ever been."

Doc pauses for a moment.

"I've been thinking. I happen to have $480 from my Army savings that I'd like to invest in an island. Know any for sale?"

"Are you sure?" asks a surprised Wick. "How could I let you do that?"

"Wick, I'd really like to. You've done so much for me. When I came home from the war it was your mentoring that got me into this intern program. Besides, we like the same things. I couldn't think of a better partner for such an investment."

A few days later, they pay a visit to Marc Braverly, bank officer at Bank of New York.

"We are prepared to put in the down payment you indicated was required to purchase Dyer Island," says Wick.

"Very good," Marc replies. "Once the funds have cleared, we will be in touch with the seller to initiate a contract. Of course, there will also be a title search."

"Sounds good," says Wick. "How long do you anticipate this will take?"

"It's probably pretty straightforward," says Marc. "But Washington County, Maine might pose additional requirements."

A week later, Marc is on the telephone with Wick.

"Regarding the Dyer Island sale, the county is requiring some documentation that shows the island is not being purchased for commercial development. If you plan a business enterprise, the tax assessment will be significantly higher then it is presently."

"We just plan to use it for recreation," replies Wick.

"Okay," says Marc. "A notarized statement to that effect will be required. Then we can move forward right away."

"Pleased to hear," says Wick. "We'd like to act on this quickly."

A couple of weeks later, Wick and Doc celebrate over lunch at a New York City cafe. A waiter uncorks a bottle of champagne and pours two glasses.

"Special occasion, gentlemen?" he asks.

"We just bought an island," offers Doc.

"Sight unseen, off the coast of Maine," echoes Wick.

Wick and Doc raise their glasses and Wick offers a toast.

"Here's to my friend, colleague, and fellow land baron."

"Here's to my friend, colleague, and fellow adventurer."

They clink their glasses as Doc offers a compliment. "I didn't realize you were such a savvy negotiator."

"They really wanted to get rid of it," says Wick. "Twenty-five dollars a month for four years is manageable but a big chunk of your Army savings is also a big commitment."

They pause for a moment in thought as they take another sip.

"Did we make the right decision?" asks Wick.

"You bet we did," replies Doc. "And what if we didn't? There is something liberating about being the purveyors of our fate. I think we're very lucky, Wick."

Chapter Four
The First Adventure

I t's early June and Wick and Doc are about to visit their island which, so far, they've only seen through photographs. They've both managed to arrange a full week of vacation which really amounts to nine days. Since they need to acquire camping gear and supplies along the way, it is impractical for them to travel by bus. Wick borrows a 1941 Packard woody station wagon from Roosevelt Hospital. It's rugged and has ample room to carry any gear they might need. Travel by road is slow. They leave Manhattan at 4 a.m. but it takes them nearly six hours to go from New York City to Boston where they stop at a U.S. Army surplus store.

"This store brings me bittersweet memories from the war," admits Doc. "But it's the best and cheapest gear for our purposes."

"Yes," agrees Wick. "We can probably find just about everything that's on our list."

The doctors purchase folding shovels and other tools, two canteens with belts to carry water, a pair of binoculars, a canvas bag filled with cooking gear, two duffel bags with handles and shoulder straps, a backpack, flashlights, rain slickers, two long machete knives for cutting through brush in rugged terrain and, most importantly, a small army tent with a built-in floor. The tent is complete with poles that come in half for portability.

The drive from Boston on winding, local roads takes them nearly nine hours. When they arrive in the DownEast town of Milbridge it is nearly dark.

"I hope we can find a place to spend the night," says Wick.

"Fear not," exclaims Doc as he spots the Milbridge Inn, a quaint old house that displays a vacancy sign. "Any place will do, and this should do us nicely," he adds.

Wick drives the woody into the parking lot and the two go in. A man reading a newspaper is sitting in an armchair next to a big, welcoming fireplace.

Wick looks around and sees no one else in the room. "Can we obtain a room for the night?" he asks.

The man looks up from his paper, rings a bell which is on the table next to him, and goes back to his paper. In comes Doreen, an elderly lady dressed quite plainly in pants and a heavy sweater, wearing a rugged smile.

"Don't mind him," she says. "He's not much of a talker. Are you looking for a room?"

"That would be nice," says Wick. "Just for one night. We're heading for Dyer Island."

Wick pulls out a map and points to the tiny island next to several others across Narraguagus Bay.

"Oh, that's owned by a paper company. Nobody lives there. Are you sure about where you are going?" she asks.

"Yes ma'am," replies Wick. "The paper company sold it, and we're the new owners. We're hoping we can find someone to take us over."

"That's across from Wyman's Landing," says Doreen. "It's a two-mile crossing but you won't find any water taxis. There are only fishermen here."

"Perhaps we could rent a rowboat?" poses Doc.

"I'll be happy to call the man who runs the marina next to Wyman's canning factory," says Doreen. "But they won't be open until the morning. How about I set you up with a room and I'll give them a call first thing in them morning?"

"We'd greatly appreciate that," says Wick.

The young doctors follow Doreen up a creaky staircase to a second-floor hallway where she opens the door to the first room to the right. The room is simple with two single beds and a large dresser and a lamp on a table between the beds. A window looks out across the bay. The room is musty and smells of salt water.

"This will be just fine," says Doc.

"Okay boys," says Doreen. "The Red Barn just a quarter mile down the road serves a good breakfast. By that time, I will have checked to see if Walter Sturgis might be able to arrange a boat."

"Much appreciated," replies Wick.

Wick and Doc open the window as wide as it can go, retrieve some overnight things from the woody, flop down on the beds, and fall asleep before they can even undress for the night. The next morning, they awake at 6 a.m. and notice a note has been placed under the door. Doc picks it up.

"It's from Doreen," says Doc who reads it out loud. "'I was able to speak with Walter Sturgis. He's the man who runs Wyman's Landing where several fishmen keep their boats. He'll arrange for a rowboat that's seaworthy enough to get you across. It's five dollars a week and you can pay the man at the dock when you get there.'"

After breakfast at The Red Barn, Wick and Doc return to the Inn to settle with Doreen.

"Thanks for your hospitality and help," says Wick. "How do we get to Wyman's Landing?"

"Head down the road to the right," she says, "and in a mile you'll turn right onto Wyman Road. The Landing is a mile and a half down Wyman on the left."

Following Doreen's directions, Wick and Doc arrive at Wyman's landing at 8:30 a.m. They notice the gangplank from the pier to the dock is at a very steep angle. Milbridge is far up the coast of Maine bordering Canada's Maritime Provinces and known for its ocean tides which are among the highest on earth and can rise or fall as much as twelve feet twice a day. That's why below the pier at Wyman's Marina, boats are moored at a floating dock.

After paying the man at the office and carrying their supplies down the steep incline, the two young doctors prepare to get into the rental rowboat for the two-mile crossing to Dyer Island. It's a calm and clear day. The boat has two sets of oars and a navigation compass in the stern. They have loaded their camping supplies, but Wick expresses second thoughts about their mode of transportation.

"We can hardly even see it from here," observes Wick. "Are you sure this is a good idea?"

"What could go wrong?" replies Doc confidently.

A dock hand with a thick Maine accent is helping them get oriented.

"Just keep the compass at one hundred ten degrees," he says. "You'll hit land at a small dock where the lobsterman's shack is. It ain't much, so keep a keen eye out for it. Hope you men are in good shape."

Wick and Doc make an awkward start rowing across Narraguagus Bay. Managing oars is not something these doctors had any practice in. They work up a good sweat and as time passes, Dyer Island comes into closer view. As they close in, they see the island is lined with evergreen trees behind a rocky coastline. They hear the bell from a nautical channel marker as Doc stops rowing to take a better look.

"Isn't it beautiful? It looks like the trees have grown back."

"And there's the shack!" says Wick with excitement.

The two do-it-yourself sailors row awkwardly up to a weathered dock and Doc jumps off to get a line around a mooring, and then another. Wick gets out and they walk up the gangplank to the badly weathered pier. As they step onto the rocky soil, Wick bends down to touch it.

"At long last, Dyer Island," he exclaims as though he were a conqueror.

Their road to buy this island wasn't as easy as they had thought it would be. During the title search there were exchanges of letters as county officials were wary of any significant development plans. One letter informed them that the taxes would be reassessed if there were plans to build on the island. Wick and Doc were both required to sign affidavits stating they had no plans for commercial development to maintain a low tax levy.

As the two shake hands and share a manly hug, there is a grunt from a man standing nearby who operates the lobster boat in the cove that neither Wick nor Doc had noticed. It is Glenn Flynn. The slim man is dressed in overalls under waterproof hip boots held up with suspenders. He looks to be in his forties, a cigarette dangling from the corner of his mouth. He's a third-generation lobsterman and like most native Mainers, he displays an element of distrust when it comes to the motives of outsiders. He speaks through his cigarette in a crusty Maine accent.

"Better tie 'er up a little tighter, boys," he says referring to their rowboat moored down below. "These tides can get a bit wicked. You boys must be the ones who bought the island. I'm Glenn Flynn and I fish in these waters."

Wick and Doc move over quickly to greet him.

"Just so you know," he adds, "I still have lobster rights here."

Doc reaches out to shake Glenn's hand. "Pleased to meet you," declares Doc. "I'm Meredith Jones and this is Walter Wickson."

Wick also extends his hand but Glenn ignores it.

"Of course," replies Doc, "you are welcome to use this island as you have. We're not here to make waves. We plan to set up a camp and walk around for a few days to see what's what."

"Well, there's lots of wildlife here," responds Glenn. "Hardly any deer, no bears that I know of but lots of small animals and birds. You'll find blueberries soon in the fields above the east coast. I come by early in the morning and late in the afternoon. You can use the shack as your camp."

"We appreciate your hospitality," replies Wick as Glenn looks at his watch.

"You'll have to excuse me. Got a catch to bring back."

Glenn unties from the mooring and boards his lobster boat, starts the diesel engine and heads out.

"He sure does speak his mind," observes Wick.

"He's a classic Mainer," says Doc. "He says what he means and means what he says."

The young doctors spend the next hour pitching their tent, readying their sleeping gear, and building a fire with dry branches they gather as the sun is going down. They dine on sandwiches they brought as darkness sets in.

Morning arrives to the sound of birds in a singing frenzy. Doc has refreshed the fire. There is a pot of coffee on a rack placed over it and Wick is now filling a couple of tin cups as Glenn arrives on his morning rounds.

"Mornin'," says Glenn as he walks from the pier. "Hope you boys had a good night."

He pulls a map out of his pocket and presents it to Doc, pointing out some spots as he unfolds it. "You asked about the island. There's a cove north 'a here 'bout a half mile up. Great spot for a new pier. Pretty rugged terrain all around though."

Wick points to a spot on the map. "Is that Nova Scotia just across the water?"

"Just a stone's throw," replies Glenn. "But you don't want to attempt that crossing."

"Why?" asks Wick.

"Beyond this bay, those are some of the meanest waters a sailor can encounter. The tides over there also rise and fall as much as forty feet."

"Thanks for the warning," replies Doc. "We'll just stick to the island."

"We were also wondering if you know why the island was named Dyer?" Wick asks.

"Don't know precisely," replies Glenn. "But there's been a history of boats stranded during storms. We get some mean ones, causing you might say dire situations. Get it?" He chuckles.

"Can you join us for coffee?" offers Wick.

Glenn ignores the invitation. "Gotta get on to the pots, boys," he says as he heads back to his boat. He cranks up his diesel and he's off.

Wick and Doc pack lunches into their army surplus backpack and walk north looking for the cove Glenn mentioned. Doc consults a compass as well as the map Glenn gave them as they navigate through the woods, swatting at insects and cutting the brush with their machetes. They finally spot a cove like the one Glenn mentioned and Doc points it out.

"There it is! Just like Glenn described."

"And it's perfect!" adds Wick.

They continue to explore by heading through the woods and reach a clearing on the other side of the island. They emerge from the woods and see an open field with spring flowers and wild blueberry bushes. The clearing goes all the way to the rocky shore where waves crash and create quite a mist in front of the blue water. A wide assortment of sea birds dive into the mist to catch fish. In the distance, more small islands off the mainland coast look the same from their vantage point, and, as they learned, the rough waters leading to Nova

Scotia. As they focus back on land, a stiff breeze creates waves over the field of bushes before them and they hear the sound of clangs from a nautical channel marker in Narraguagus Bay.

Wick and Doc stop and breathe deeply while taking it all in.

"Just think," says Doc. "This summer the blueberries will be ripe, and we'll be feasting on them among the birds and butterflies."

The two decide to split up, following the shore in different directions and meeting back at the fisherman's shack to share their experiences. Doc heads clockwise and Wick the other way. It might have been a simple idea but it's a complicated island. The shore is ragged and leads each down unplanned paths. Neither Wick nor Doc make it back on time after seemingly walking in circles. Three hours later, they reunite.

"A thousand acres is far bigger than I visualized," says Doc.

"And like a whole bunch of dead-end streets," says Wick.

"But beautiful streets at that," adds Doc.

Chapter Five
Harry's Reckoning

Ten days later, inside a juvenile courtroom in New York City, Harry sits nervously next to his court-appointed attorney. Thelma Thompson, Wick, and Doc sit in the gallery. A court officer announces the arrival of the judge.

"All rise for his honor Judge Thomas Wysinger."

Everyone stands as Judge Wysinger, an experienced former trial attorney of about forty, is seated on the bench and ruffles through some papers.

"The first case before me is that of Harold Thompson. Please come forward."

Harry and his attorney walk up to the defendant's stand.

"It says here you broke into a grocery store. How do you plead?"

Harry responds with a weak voice. "I didn't break in for food or anything..."

"Mr. Thompson," the judge interrupts, "you must speak up so the court can hear you."

Harry tries again after nervously shuffling his feet and looking at his attorney. "I didn't steal food or anything. In fact, it wasn't locked. I was just taking the empty bottles."

"Well," demands judge Wysinger, "you must plead either guilty or not guilty."

Thelma shakes her head and looks at Wick, then covers her face with her hands.

This time, the court-appointed attorney takes over for Harry. "My client pleads guilty with an explanation, your honor."

"I must enter that as guilty," the judge responds.

Thelma can't hold back her emotions.

"Oh no, he's a good boy!" she says out loud as she looks down and shakes her head.

Wick tries to comfort her by putting his hand on her shoulder.

The judge taps his gavel. "I will not tolerate any outbursts from the gallery," he warns.

"I must also consider past behavior," he continues as he looks through some papers. "Even though an earlier charge of robbery at knife point was dropped, this court must recognize prior activity."

Thelma is upset and in tears but covers her mouth as she sobs silently.

"I have no choice therefore," the judge continues, "to remand you to Lavenburg Juvenile Detention Center for sixty days, after which you will serve three months' probation and take part in the Big Brothers program."

Judge Wysinger gavels for the next case as Harry is led away by a court officer. He looks at his mother and shakes his head. Thelma tries to follow them but is stopped by another court officer as Harry is walked out of the chamber to a holding room.

Wick and Doc leave the courthouse while Thelma stays behind to speak with Harry's attorney. Wick expresses his disappointment. "I'm surprised the judge didn't go easier on Harry and let him off the hook."

"I was reading about that judge," replies Doc. "People have said he has a reputation for going hard on Negro boys. It's a real shame and it's really unfair. The judge just sees Harry's face and stereotypes him."

As they continue walking, Doc's face is turning red as he gets worked up about the situation. "They don't even consider the circumstances around a young man who lost his father in the war. A real hero he was! And what does the system do for Harry?"

"I wish there was a way we could reach the judge," says Wick.

"Well, it's just not fair," adds Doc. "Think about it. Here we are about to start a life of privilege, owning an island of all things, and boys like Harry can't even get a small break."

"Maybe we can connect the dots," ponders Wick, "between the island and Harry."

The two continue walking now in silence as they pass spring flowers growing in the small, urban gardens along the Manhattan sidewalk.

Chapter Six
Connections

Anne is lying flat on her back in a hospital bed in the tuberculosis ward at Bellevue Hospital. The table next to her bed is stacked with papers and books. There is a knock and Wick enters wearing a surgical mask and holding a bouquet of flowers.

"Hello Dr. Dobson. I heard you were here and wanted to see how you are doing."

Anne is surprised and excited to see him. "Dr. Wickson!"

"Please just call me Wick."

"And please just call me Anne. What a pleasant surprise!"

Back on the path at Camp Dyer, as older Harry and elderly Wick continue their walk with Johnny in the woods, Wick recalls that visit with Anne fifty-one years earlier.

"When I was visiting Anne that day," says Wick, "the thoughts Doc and I had about what to do with this island were changing. Of course, we had no idea at the time Anne and I would someday be married, but she had a determined vision of the direction Doc and I were heading when it came to the island."

The three stop at a cabin along the path. Harry moves off the path to take a closer look while Wick and Johnny stay on the path. All the cabins on the island bear the names of the original campers who built them and this one is named Harry's Cabin. He rejoins the other two with a sparkle in his eyes.

"This is another special place to me," says Harry, "and there is no doubt in my mind that Anne had a profound influence on why it was built."

Flashing back after Wick's first visit with Anne in the tuberculosis ward, Wick and Doc are having lunch at the Roosevelt Hospital cafeteria, discussing Anne's situation. Wick wonders how Anne can handle the situation with such grace.

"I simply can't imagine what it would be like to go through what Anne is having to endure."

"She's one tough lady," offers Doc. "She certainly put my smoking habit into perspective. How is she managing to do all the reading she is doing?"

"It isn't easy," says Wick. "The books are heavy and hard to manage."

"Let me think about that," offers Doc. "I might be able to build something to help her with the mechanics. Dealing with that confinement must be extraordinarily difficult."

"Confinement is the one thing she now has in common with Harry," says Wick, "but the situations could not be more different."

"Absolutely," agrees Doc. "But her life is on the line through no fault of her own, while Harry is up against a system that's stacked against him because of the color of his skin. Without his dad on the scene, he needs a role model. And I can't get his dad off my mind. I'm still trying to trace the Negro soldier who saved my life. It occurs to me that maybe the reason I can't find records about him is that he was killed in battle. The burning question is could he have possibly been the soldier who saved my life?"

"That would be an astronomical coincidence," admits Wick.

Doc is silent for a few moments as he thinks things over. "What if we could figure out a way to bring Harry to the island?" he wonders.

"I'm not sure how we could manage that," replies Wick. "What kind of liability would we be faced with? And, more importantly, he's under court-ordered detention. Would his mom even approve?"

"Why don't you present that possibility to her?" asks Doc.

"I do plan on visiting Thelma tomorrow evening," replies Wick. "How about joining me? And we could ask that question together."

Wick and Doc are sitting on a couch in Thelma's apartment as she brings them tea. Beside them is the table with a picture of Harry's father along with a folded American flag and medals. Doc is taking a keen interest in them.

"What was your husband's name?" asks Doc.

"Corporal Harold S. Thompson," replies Thelma. "He was a tank gunner when he was killed in Burma."

"When was that?" asks Doc.

"Four years ago last April."

"I was stationed in India and on detail in Burma at that very time," says Doc.

He admires the medals, which include two purple hearts and a distinguished service cross.

"The distinguished service cross is right up there with the medal of honor," Doc marvels. "Did you get any details about what happened?"

"He shot a Japanese soldier who was involved in a fire fight," offers Thelma. "He saved some of the men he was with, but couldn't save himself."

"So sorry," says Doc. "It's men like your husband who brought me a great deal of inspiration."

"Does Harry realize what his father did?" asks Wick.

"Oh yes. But it was too much for an eleven-year-old boy to take in. And things have gone downhill for him ever since. For one thing, Harry is terrified about neighborhood gangs. He says he was threatened by a member of the Dragons."

"Any serious encounters?" asks Wick.

"Not yet," says Thelma. "But he was also approached by the Sportsmen. They want him to join and he wants nothing to do with any of them, thank God."

"I know he's under court confinement," says Wick. "But what if we could persuade the judge to allow Harry to stay on our island this summer?"

At Lavenburg, Harry is sullen and depressed. He stays in his room as much as he can and has no desire to talk with any of the other boys. He thinks of his late father, his mom, and Roseanne. He digs into his pocket and pulls out the dog tag that identified his dad and holds it tightly in his hand.

I don't belong in this place, he thinks. *I didn't hurt anybody. I was just trying to make some money and help Roseanne. We deserve more. If this is the kind of life I'm stuck with, I don't want to continue.*

Later, Harry sits in the visitation room with a social worker, Thelma, Wick, and Doc. Wick is pitching an idea that might help Harry.

"Dr. Jones and I own an island off the coast of Maine. What would you think about spending the summer there?"

"It might be a good change for you," agrees Thelma.

"The judge might shorten your time here if you agree to temporary custody with the doctors," the social worker echoes.

"I'd rather go home," replies Harry who is not thrilled.

"That's not possible," says the social worker. "The judge won't allow you to go home until you've been through a program."

"If Judge Wysinger agrees," adds Doc, "you could be released from here early and go home after your time on the island at the end of the summer. And you'll be working on island projects. In fact, we will pay you six dollars a week for your efforts."

The job aspect in the offer peaks Harry's attention but he doesn't admit it.

"Could I take two of my birds?" asks Harry.

"Your birds?" asks a puzzled Wick.

"I have pigeons," explains Harry. "Two are special ones. I call them long birds. Somebody's feeding 'em while I'm away, but I'm the only one they fly for."

Wick looks at Doc who nods with approval.

"I don't think that would be a problem," replies Wick.

Back at his apartment a week later, Wick opens the day's mail. There is a letter from New York Juvenile Court. After opening it, he smiles and picks up the telephone to call Doc.

"I just got a letter from the court," says Wick. "We have been granted custody of Harry for the summer."

"That's great news," says Doc on the other end of the phone line. "But will the judge let him stay on the island by himself during the days we can't be there?"

"Yes," replies Wick. "The judge knows that our experiment with Harry depends on his fending for himself during the days we can't be present. We stipulated that he would have everything he needs and would not leave the island except for an emergency."

"Good," says Doc. "I think we really should do what we can to help the boy. You know, I'm still trying to find out who the soldier was who saved my life in Burma. The more I check, the more likely it could have been Harry's father."

"You really think?" asks Wick.

"Whether it's true or not, believing it actually makes me feel doubly sure we're doing the right thing."

It's evening in the Bellevue Hospital TB ward where Wick is visiting with Anne. Doc enters after knocking.

"Good evening, doctors."

He is pushing a contraption on wheels that looks like a hospital bed table with a bookstand and moveable mirrors. Anne looks puzzled.

"Hello Doc. What is that?"

"My invention," pronounces Doc. "This will let you do your reading upside down without having to hold up heavy books."

Doc demonstrates.

"You. Put the book here, upside down. The end of the book is on your left and the beginning on the right."

Doc places one of Anne's books on the table, moves it over to Anne's bed, and moves the mirrors around, lining them up behind her point of view.

"Can you read it?" he asks.

Anne looks and nods yes as Doc continues his instructions.

"Now, turn the page to the right."

Anne does it and smiles.

"It works! How did you figure that out?"

"Well," says Doc boastfully, "I have a motto. The difficult I do at once. The impossible takes longer." He gives a snarky chuckle as if making fun of what he just said.

"That is amazing!" exclaims Anne. "Thank you so much."

Harry is in the visitation room at Lavenburg, sitting across from his half sister Roseanne at a table that divides the room. Roseanne is thin and pale but having a better day health wise than when Harry tried to visit her.

"How'd you get away from the apartment?" asks Harry.

"They let me go for a walk. I feel much better when I go outside. But I've got to get back soon. I heard about what happened and I'm worried for you."

"I'm okay," replies Harry, "but they want to send me to an island."

"An island?" she asks.

"It's in Maine. No place I wanna go."

"Maine is near Canada," says Roseanne. "I hear it's beautiful." She is looking at the clock. "I gotta go in a minute or they'll get mad," she says.

"All they want is the monthly check," protests Harry. "You need to get out of there."

"That's impossible," she says.

"They won't even take you to the doctor," pleads Harry. "They should know you need to see a doctor."

"They say I have asthma," replies Roseanne, "and it's all in my head."

"I say it ain't in your head," argues Harry. "You need to see a doctor."

"They say they don't have the money."

Harry has been waiting for a chance to tell Roseanne about the money he has been stowing away near his pigeons behind the loose bricks.

"I've been saving some money," says Harry. "There's enough for you to see a doctor. It's hidden on the roof near my birds. There's a map of exactly where it is, folded under the left rear corner of the loft. Promise you'll see a doctor."

"I've got to go," says Roseanne as she rushes out without giving him an answer.

Roseanne knows that Harry is right about her situation, but is afraid to confront her foster parents. Ely and Susan Jones are both collecting welfare checks and managed to persuade someone in Social Services that they should be foster parents. They treat Roseanne as though she were a pet kept in a cage. They provide her three meals a day but don't help her pursue any interests. Roseanne has created her own world in her room. On her good days, she manages to pick up magazines with her small allowance at a nearby drug store. Her biggest joy is checking out books from the library. But she has no interest in doing anything when her lungs tighten up and she struggles to breathe.

Harry is right, she thinks. *Maybe I should try to see a doctor on my own.*

Chapter Seven
Harry's Adventure

W ick, Doc, and Thelma are loading Harry's things into the back of a woody station wagon in front of Harry's apartment building. It's the same 1941 Packard they used on their first trip. Wick has managed to purchase it from Roosevelt Hospital at a good price because it was due to be replaced by a new one. Thelma is all smiles, as if to display the relief she is feeling that something positive is happening for Harry. Harry is wearing a US Army issued jacket that belonged to his father and carrying a cage that holds two of his pigeons.

"I'm afraid Harry doesn't have the right clothes," Thelma says apologetically. "He has some of his father's rugged clothes from the army."

"Don't worry," assures Wick. "We've got some extra things and we'll do a little shopping along the way."

He calls to Harry. "Harry, do you have all of your things?"

"I think so," Harry replies.

"Go ahead and make yourself comfortable in the back seat while I speak with your mother," replies Wick.

"Harry's never been away from home," says Thelma anxiously.

"He'll be fine," assures Wick. "We'll be with him on the island for the first ten days," says Doc. "Then we hope to line up a local fisherman we met to check on Harry's progress daily before we return on the following weekend. We've also connected with a local doctor in Milbridge in case Harry should have any medical needs."

Wick and Doc get in the car as Thelma goes to the window where Harry is sitting behind Wick in the driver's seat.

"Harry, you take good care of yourself and do what the doctors say. I love you." Thelma is in tears and waves as they drive off.

The woody wagon travels north up the West Side Highway, through the Bronx, and then northeast through Connecticut and follows the coastal route toward Maine. This time, the doctors won't make a stop in Boston, following a more direct route north. Inside, Wick and Doc discuss their plans once they arrive in Milbridge, for the boat ride from Wyman's Landing to Dyer Island.

"You called Glenn Flynn, right?" Doc asks.

"Yep," replies Wick. "Everybody knows everybody in Milbridge. I got his number from Town Hall."

"Good," says Doc. "Just hope we don't break down on the way."

"Needn't be concerned," Wick responds with a chuckle. "This six-year-old wagon is built like a tank."

Harry reaches back to take the cover off his caged pigeons.

"Are your birds okay?" asks Doc.

"They don't like to be covered during the day," replies Harry. "They wanna see where they're goin'."

Harry is now silent as he ponders what's in store. He has mixed feelings about leaving home and his mother who always provides moral support. He's not used to getting things he wants but always gets what he needs even though they struggle over money.

As the skylines of cities in Connecticut pass by and morph into country scenes, Harry is deep in thought. He thinks about the bleak and bland events that mark his daily life. He's supposed to play by the rules, he thinks, but everyone else seems to break the rules to get ahead. He doesn't have any real friends, people who might share his interests. He'd like to build things and help other people but doesn't know where to start. There's a yearning to find purpose in his life, but what is his purpose other than being a prisoner of the life he has?

Time passes until Wick breaks the ice.

"So Harry, what do you think of the countryside?"

"It's big," says Harry. "But there aren't many people."

"Oh, there are lots of people," retorts Doc. "But they're spread out."

"Lonely people?" asks Harry.

"Sometimes," replies Wick. "But not more than city people. You can be lonely even in a crowded place. On Dyer Island I don't feel lonely at all."

"How can that be?" replies Harry.

"You'll find out," offers Doc. "Without the noise of the city, you can actually hear the animals speaking to one another."

"Yeah, right," says Harry. He pauses, thinking about it. "Some of the guys in my neighborhood brag a lot. I think they're the loneliest people in the world."

The woody wagon passes a Welcome to Milbridge sign and they drive south down Wyman Road. A rocky coastline juts out to the left behind modest homes and other waterfront properties. A strong salt water smell and constant chatter of seagulls permeates the car. They pull into the parking lot of Wyman's Landing where Wick and Doc launched their rental rowboat earlier in the spring. Glenn Flynn emerges from his lobster boat, which is docked at the pier. He has agreed to take them and their supplies two miles across the sound to the fisherman's shack on Dyer Island. He was reluctant at first, but realized keeping a close eye on what was going on with the island was the better option. He waves as Wick, Doc, and Harry approach.

"Good timing," hollers Wick. "How's the fishing been?"

"Can't complain," replies Glenn. "How was your drive up?"

"We had good company," replies Wick. "And I hope we didn't keep you waiting. This is Harry Thompson, the young man I was telling you about."

Harry offers a half-hearted wave and nod.

"This is Sean, my helper," says Glenn as he introduces the young man who assists him on the boat.

They all begin to carry supplies from the woody wagon to the boat down a steep gangplank at low tide.

"There seems to be enough food here to feed an army," observes Wick. "You packed cheese, smoked meat, and Russian pastries from Zabar's?"

"My favorite deli to splurge in," replies Doc. "I figure if we're going to rough it, we're going to eat in style."

Doc does have quite the appetite as Wick observed him recently consume a sixteen ounce steak, baked potatoes, a giant bowl of pasta, and dessert for lunch one afternoon. There was no salad, which Doc refers to as rabbit food.

After three trips, all are on board and Glenn prepares to cast off as Sean, his helper, unties the lines from the moorings and jumps aboard. With the diesel fired up, they're off for the short trip across Narraguagus Bay to Dyer Island. The boat's compass holds steady at one hundred ten degrees and Wick, Doc, and Harry stand behind Glenn as he pilots. Harry's presence brings out the fatherly instincts in Glenn, who engages Harry.

"So, you're from Manhattan Island," says Glenn. "You're going from one island to a completely different one. Ever been on a lobster boat, son?"

"No," replies Harry.

The cool breeze from the water gets more intense as the boat picks up speed, navigating through lobster trap markers floating on the bay.

"What are those things floating in the water?" asks Harry.

"Those are floating markers attached to lobster traps," replies Glenn. "I'll show you."

Glenn cuts the engine and reverses it slightly to stop next to one of the markers. He pulls the float out of the water and describes the markings to Harry.

"The floats are coded by color and number," says Glenn whose hands have become somewhat animated by the question. "They are tied to a cage on the bottom that is baited to attract lobsters. This one does not belong to me so I won't pull it up. At least once a day we check mine to see what we caught. The lobsters that are too small I put back in the water to allow them to grow up. It's the law here in Maine. Ever eaten lobster, son?"

"No," replies Harry.

"Well then, you're in for a real treat when you do," he boasts.

Glenn puts the trap marker back into the water and they resume their short trip. He cautiously slows his boat as they approach the dock by the small pier near the fisherman's shack. His assistant jumps off as Glenn cuts the engine and tosses him the lines. Once on the dock, Glenn demonstrates to Harry how one of the lines is correctly tied to a mooring. With the boat secure, they begin to unload and climb up the steep gangplank at low tide. Harry carries his cage with his pigeons and puts it onto a weathered picnic table off the pier and next to the shack.

"Give us a hand with the other things, Harry," Wick shouts from the boat.

Harry joins them in carrying jugs of water and bags containing food as well as tools, sleeping bags, and a large, heavy folded canvas. As the last of their supplies is removed from Glenn's boat, Wick and Doc wave to Glenn and Sean as they move out for their afternoon rounds. Doc moves over to the large, folded canvas.

"Harry, this is our tent. Help me move it over to the flat spot near the picnic table."

The Army surplus tent is very heavy and awkward to carry. Once in place, they unfold it and line up the posts and stakes. Wick now joins the effort to raise the tent, tie down the corners, and pound stakes into the ground to stabilize it. After a while, the three manage to create a campsite near the fisherman's shack and picnic table. Doc starts a campfire in a pit he fashioned out of stones. Later, they heat a simple meal of canned pork and beans with frankfurters on a rack placed over the fire. Doc brings two pans from the fire to the picnic table and dinner is served on tin camping plates. As the three gobble up the food, Harry takes time out to feed his birds with seeds he has brought. He places a pan of water into the cage and covers it as the sun is setting.

The next morning, Doc is the first to rise at daylight and refreshes the campfire. A pot of coffee is soon percolating over the fire and there are pastries stacked on a plate. Birds and other wildlife are making quite a racket. Wick is now up but Harry still sleeps in his sleeping bag before getting a wakeup call from Wick who offers him a tin of coffee.

"Morning Harry," says Wick. "Time to get up. We've got a big day ahead of us."

Harry is not a morning person and doesn't speak a word but slowly gets out of his sleeping bag and sits on the picnic table with the tin of coffee.

"Sorry Harry, no milk," replies Wick as he places a small tin of sugar on the table next to Harry.

After packing some peanut butter and jelly sandwiches, the three head out to make their way along a rugged path through the woods close to the western shore heading north. Wick and Doc are carrying tools: a shovel, an axe, a machete knife, and a large, two-man saw. Harry has a bundle of other things strapped to his back as he struggles with his footing. The machete comes in handy as Doc leads the way, creating a crude path. They continue to the cove Wick and Doc visited earlier and head up to a spot that had been cleared by the paper company. They drop their loads and Doc sizes up the lay of the land.

"This will be a great spot for a cabin," he announces.

Back in New York, Anne is flat on her back reading in her room in the Bellevue Hospital tuberculosis ward. Dr. Shaw walks in with a broad smile on his face.

"Anne, I have very good news. Your infection has not materialized as we had feared. So we are recommending you be transferred to Trudeau in Saranac Lake as soon as possible."

"That's wonderful!" she responds.

"You'll still be on your back for a while," he warns. "But you will gradually be sitting up as they monitor your progress."

"I can't wait!" exclaims Anne. "How soon?"

"How's tomorrow?" replies Dr. Shaw.

"My bags are already packed," jokes Anne. "Let's get on with it."

On Dyer Island, near the cove they visited earlier, Doc is laying out the exact spot for the cabin with four sticks and twine marking four corners.

"We'll need lumber for the cabin," he declares. "But we can begin by making our own rough timbers from the woods."

The three would-be woodsmen get busy with a population of Norway Spruces. They're not more than twelve inches in diameter at the base. Doc shows Harry how to notch a tree with an axe. Wick and Doc demonstrate the use of the two-man saw. Then Harry takes Doc's place. They are sawing opposite the notch they cut with the axe and slightly above it so the tree will fall in the direction of the notch. As the first tree falls, Harry runs for cover while Doc and Wick laugh.

"Good job Harry," praises Wick. "You just cut your first tree."

Doc then shows Harry how to cut another tree with only the axe. A deep notch is made on one side and then another deeper notch above it on the other side until the tree falls.

By the next day, several trees have been cut and Harry is learning to use a spudding tool to remove the bark after branches have been removed. As work continues over the next three days, there are now more than a dozen trees on the ground and several of them turned into logs ready for cabin construction.

At the end of the third day, Harry is once again sending his birds into flight with a whistle. Each pigeon soars high into the air and makes wide circles before Harry brings it back with another whistle.

On the morning of day ten, with Wick and Doc set to head back to New York, Harry is up early making coffee on a newly acquired kerosene stove in the fisherman's shack. While Wick and Doc are still sleeping it is Harry who wakes them up.

"Time to get up, doctors," calls Harry with two cups of coffee in hand.

"Morning, Harry," responds Wick. "I see you've taken over breakfast chores."

"Glenn will be coming soon," replies Harry. "Then I'll be in charge."

Doc accepts the second cup from Harry. "Good morning, Harry. You are hereby appointed captain of the island."

After breakfast, Wick and Doc have a private conversation with Glenn aboard his boat before departing. Glenn is concerned about their plans leaving Harry to fend for himself.

"I appreciate you payin' me to check on the boy," says Glenn, "but I can't be responsible for his well bein'. I checked with a town selectman who says you have to have a plan in place."

Wick hands Glenn a large envelope which he opens.

"And that's why we wanted to make sure you have all of this in case," replies Wick. "This has the contact information for our friend who is a doctor at the Milbridge Clinic. He knows exactly what do to in an emergency and has the resources to handle it. We've also included our private telephone numbers if you should need to reach us."

"Harry has everything he needs," adds Doc. "We have been given special permission from a New York court to create this special program for Harry."

Glenn is going through the papers.

"It looks like you've thought of everything," he says. "I'll do what I can for the boy but I'm not sure I agree with what you're doin'."

Wick and Doc have loaded all their personal things onto Glenn's boat after unloading more food and supplies for Harry. It's a tense moment for them as leaving Harry on the island is a point of no return in their bold experiment.

"Well Harry," says Doc. "The ball is in your court. We'll be back in six days and Glenn will be checking in every day."

"Cutting and spudding trees by yourself is pretty ambitious," adds Wick. "Don't push yourself too hard or take any risks. And remember to turn off the kerosene stove when you're finished cooking."

"I can do that," assures Harry.

"Make yourself useful in any ways you want," adds Doc. "And take time to explore."

Harry waves as Wick and Doc depart with Glenn and his helper. As the sound of Glenn's boat fades, Harry is now truly alone for the first time in his life. There is only the sound of clangs from the nautical channel marker in the distance to break the silence as Harry sits and contemplates the moment. After a few minutes, Harry gets up and walks around the encampment he and the two doctors had created. He puts some more wood on the fire, looks out over the water, and lets out a primal shout.

"Hey you Dragons! You can't touch me now!"

More silence. Harry visits his pigeons, sends them up with whistles and back again with another. Then more silence with only the sounds of some birds chirping and gentle waves washing up on the shore. It's a restive and peaceful time.

As darkness falls, Harry is on his back in his sleeping bag near the campfire. There are sounds of an owl hooting and then a reply. Crickets chirp back and forth as though they are talking to one another. Frogs croak to each other.

The doctors were right, he thinks to himself as he falls asleep. *They are talking to each other.*

Chapter Eight
Next Steps

In New York City, Roseanne is alone on the roof of her foster parents' apartment building where Harry keeps the pigeons that remain in his loft. She feeds the birds with seeds Harry gave her and tops off their water with a soda bottle filled with tap water. She is thinking about what Harry said about money he has saved and pulls bricks out of the wall where Harry told her he hid his can of money. She finds the can, but it is empty. She carefully puts the can and bricks back. As she heads down the steps back to her apartment, she walks past a man she often sees drinking from a bottle in a paper bag.

"Hey Roseanne," he says. "What's up?"

She ignores him just like Harry did earlier and as she passes by, the man displays a mischievous smile.

At Trudeau Sanitarium in Saranac Lake, Anne is reclining on a huge sun porch with other TB patients. They are lined up against the wall facing the sun with the lake in the background. She is covered in a blanket, just like the others, writing a letter.

Four days later, Wick is reading that letter in his apartment.

"Dear Wick. I arrived at Trudeau yesterday. Dr. Simpson was so kind to arrange everything so efficiently. I am thrilled I am able to sit up much of the time. I will no longer need the reading cart that Doc was so kind to make for me. I left it at Bellevue so other patients might take advantage of it. I hope you don't find it too forward of me to ask, but I would love it if you could visit me here in Saranac Lake."

Wick smiles, pumps his fist, and says "yes" loudly to himself as he continues to read.

"It's a beautiful town and I'm sure you would enjoy the break. As the weather continues to get warmer, we patients are spending more and more time outside on the grand wraparound porch. It is most comfortable with a beautiful view of the lake. I also think you would find the medical organization here at Trudeau an interesting approach to dealing with communicable infections. Most sincerely, Anne."

Wick puts the letter down and dances around the room to imaginary music as though Anne was his partner at a grand ball.

On Dyer Island, Harry is packing lunch into a backpack. Glenn arrives from his boat carrying a bag and a small box.

"Mornin' Harry. How'd your night go?" he asks.

"Can't complain," replies Harry borrowing a phrase used by Glenn.

Glenn chuckles as he hands Harry the bag and the box. "The wife made some muffins for you. And we also want you to have what's in the box."

Harry opens the box and pulls out a flare gun.

"What is it?" asks Harry.

"It's a flare gun," explains Glenn. "And there are several shells with it."

Glenn takes it from Harry to demonstrate.

"This is how you load a flare into the gun and this is the safety switch. If the switch is off and you pull the trigger it will send up a flare that will light up the sky like the Fourth of July. If you ever need to use it, just be very careful and point it to the sky."

"Why would I use it?" asks Harry.

"It's only in case you have an emergency," responds Glenn. "Our house is on the shore. We'll be on the lookout for a flare if something bad happens and you need help."

Glenn has a fatherly air around Harry, a soft touch that is not his usual crusty demeanor around the doctors. He wants Harry to know that while he might be alone most of the time on the island, he's also got a safety net in place for him.

On day three, Harry is making great progress in his solo woodland work. He prepares to fell a tree near where others were cut earlier. Harry notches the tree with an axe and now saws on the other side above the notch with a short, two-hand saw the doctors left for him. As he has nearly cut all the way through, the weight of the tree finishes the job for him by crashing to the ground in the direction of the notch.

"Yes!" Harry celebrates, "right where I wanted it!'

That night, Harry is sitting by his campfire next to the fisherman's shack. His pigeons are covered in their cage nearby. He picks up an empty can of pork and beans with the spoon he used to eat it, to take back to the garbage inside the shack. His eyes fix on the flare gun, which he has hung on the wall. He looks inside the box below and sees several extra flares.

I wonder if it really can do what he said, Harry thinks.

He picks up the gun, loads one of the shells, and heads outside.

"Are they really looking out for a signal from me?" he asks himself.

"There are extra flares," Harry reasons, "and I bet they won't even notice."

Harry releases the safety and points the gun toward the dark sky. Then he lowers it after thinking twice. A few moments pass and Harry is now hearing a voice from an inner demon.

Are you a man or a mouse, Harry?

In a fit of misplaced courage, Harry lifts the gun up again, points it skyward, and pulls the trigger. The flare goes straight up with a whoosh and lights up the night sky.

"Wow!" he exclaims. "It is like the Fourth of July."

The display of fireworks only lasts a few seconds. Harry then puts the gun back onto the wall of the shack, goes back by the fire, and gets comfortable in his sleeping bag. He is nodding off when the sound of a boat approaches. Glenn emerges on deck, shining a powerful light on the campsite from his unmoored boat in the water only yards from the camp.

"Harry!" shouts Glenn. "We saw the flare. Are you alright?"

Harry is jolted awake and dumbstruck like a deer in headlights.

"I…I didn't think you would see it," shouts back Harry, now realizing how bad his judgement had been. "I'm sorry. I didn't mean to make you come out here."

"We'll talk later," Glenn shouts back before he navigates his boat around and once again back toward the mainland.

As the weekend approaches, Wick and Doc are on their way back to Maine. They're having lunch at a diner along the road and discussing what happened with Harry and the flare gun.

"I think Harry's curiosity just got the better of him," says Doc. "Glenn did say he was completely devastated and ashamed of what he had done."

"Adolescents sometimes do crazy things," admits Wick. "It does prove one thing."

"What's that?" asks Doc.

"That Glenn cares about Harry and meant what he said about watching out for him."

The woody station wagon is once again on the road, passes the Welcome to Milbridge sign, and pulls into the parking lot of the pier where Glenn keeps his boat. Glenn has been waiting to take the doctors back to the island. They have brought additional supplies and there is a stack of lumber waiting for them at the pier. Glenn and Sean give them a hand loading it onto the boat. A few minutes later, they arrive at the Dyer Island dock where Harry is waiting to greet them.

"Hello Harry," greets Doc. "How was your first week?"

"Good," responds Harry, "except for, you know, the flare. I promised Mr. Flynn I'd never do it again. I don't want to be like the boy and the wolf."

"Oh yes," responds Doc. "You mean the boy who cried wolf too often."

"We think you learned a lesson," adds Wick. "We'll forget about it, but you owe Glenn a debt of gratitude."

"How's the work coming?" asks Doc.

Harry perks up with excitement. "I'll show you!"

As Glenn's boat motors away, the three head for the cove construction site. The pathway has been improved with the removal of branches and other obstacles.

"I spent a whole day clearing this path," declares Harry.

As they arrive at the cabin site, there are sixteen clean logs ready for use and an additional two felled trees ready for spudding. The debris is all stacked neatly on the pile they had started earlier.

"Well, I'll be damned," exclaims Doc

"Great job, Harry," commends Wick.

The next morning, Wick, Doc, and Harry continue the work at the cabin site. Wick and Harry cut down another tree. Harry removes bark with a spudding tool after the branches are cut and removed. More logs are being stacked and ready for construction of the cabin's foundation. They mix saltwater cement in a big bucket for the footings and pour the cement into molds constructed from lumber in each of four corners and midway points between them. The first layer of the foundation comes together fashioned out of cut logs placed on the footings.

By Thursday, a frame is beginning to take shape with rough flooring constructed from planks of lumber they brought over. At the end of the day's work, as he's done every day, Harry sends his pigeons into flight with a whistle and then back again with another.

On Friday morning, Wick and Doc are boarding Glenn's boat for the return home to New York as Harry sees them off with a wave.

Anne is seated on the sun porch at Trudeau with other TB patients opening a letter from Wick. She smiles as she reads it.

"I was happy to receive your letter," writes Wick. "And I am thrilled your recovery is going so nicely. I went to visit you at Bellevue when I got back from Maine and was told of your transfer. You are very much on my mind every day. I hope to come up to visit soon even if it means missing a day on the island."

Anne plants a kiss on her fingers and touches the letter. She smiles blankly into space as though she is living in a pleasant dream.

On Dyer Island, Harry is walking on the banks of a small cove along the rocky shore and comes upon an old rowboat, which is half buried in the muck. There are also some badly weathered oars inside the boat. Harry pulls a small shovel out of his backpack, removes his shoes, and wades in to dig it out. The hull of the small boat is intact, and Harry pulls it out of the water to dry.

Later in the day, Harry rows his newfound mode of transportation back toward the camp next to the fisherman's shack. Along the way, in deeper water, he comes upon the floating marker from a lobster trap. His curiosity gets the best of him as he pulls the trap up. Inside is a good-sized lobster, which he pulls out. Harry is timid around the crustacean because of its snapping claws, and quickly drops it into the boat. *Nobody will miss one lobster*, he thinks, as he lowers the trap back into the water. A good distance away, unnoticed by Harry, a lobsterman is watching him through binoculars.

That evening, Harry has brought a large pot of water to a boil over the kerosene stove and drops the lobster in. Harry's pigeons make a mournful sound as if they sense what is happening. The lobster turns bright red as it cooks, and Harry pulls it out of the water with tongs and onto a large tin plate.

Harry sits down for his personal feast, but he has no experience with eating lobster. He is still timid about the claws. He probes them gingerly, thinking they might spring back to life. When they don't, he gets more aggressive. He breaks off the knuckle and pincer with a powerful grip of his hands. They come apart but how does he get to the meat? He quickly gives up and goes to the body of the tail which holds the most promise. The shell is stubborn and won't crack.

What is this? he thinks. *A mobster lobster?*

The only option is to find some tools. He brings the lobster to the top of a nearby stump and bangs on it with a hammer. There's a crack. Then he brings out the machete and there's a bigger crack. Back at the table, he is soon able to pull out some of the meat with a pair of pliers and a screwdriver. Then he uses a fork. Having finished the meat from the tail, he goes back to the claws. There's another trip to the stump with the hammer. A fork and a jackknife finish the job.

Harry is finally fully satisfied and now has his own lobster tale to tell.

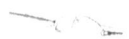

It's Friday afternoon in Saranac Lake and Anne is sitting on the sun porch with the other patients when a nurse walks up to her.

"Anne, you have a visitor."

Wick, wearing a surgical mask, appears with a bouquet of flowers.

"Oh Wick!" exclaims Anne. "I'm so glad you could come."

"You look great," says Wick.

He approaches to give Anne a hug but it is awkward.

"I'll put those flowers in a vase," offers the nurse as she takes the bouquet inside.

"I feel great, Wick. The air here is so clean. It feels good to breathe deeply again. It's also so good to see a familiar face. But I thought you were going to be in Maine this weekend."

"I am," replies Wick. "Doc is taking the train up to Lake Placid and we'll be driving to Maine first thing in the morning."

"You really went out of your way, Wick."

"I really wanted to see you."

The woody wagon once again arrives in Maine, passing the Welcome to Milbridge sign, and pulls into the pier parking lot where Glenn is waiting. Wick and Doc carry more supplies from their wagon to the pier.

"Hello Glenn," shouts Doc. "How's the fishing?"

"Can't complain," is Glenn's stock answer, but this time there is more. "Harry's turning into quite the survivor."

"How's that?" Wick asks.

"He managed to dig out an old rowboat that was grounded in one of the inlets. He's been rowing along the west shore."

Wick and Doc give each other a puzzled look and then turn to Glenn.

"We never thought about that possibility," says Doc.

As Wick and Doc get off Glenn's boat, Harry comes down to meet them. He is tan and sporting a necklace he has made from a variety of items he's gathered from the woods and the shoreline.

"How are you doing, Harry?" asks Wick.

"Good," he replies with more enthusiasm than usual. "The new logs are ready."

"With any luck," adds Doc, "we'll be finishing the rough framework before the weekend's done."

Doc points to the rowboat.

"Where did you find the boat?" he asks.

"Found it stuck in the mud near the north cove," says Harry.

"We did say make yourself useful in any ways you want," offers Wick. "But you've got to remember the court order says. You cannot leave the island."

"I promise," assures Harry.

It's a productive weekend of work for Harry and the doctors. The three raise a framework for a wall that they have built on the ground and attach it to the cabin foundation. A second, third and fourth wall follows to be raised and fastened together. Next comes a framework for the cabin's roof. Later they hang roofing shingles. Lastly comes window and door frames that were brought over on Glenn's boat. The rough work on the cabin is nearly complete except for siding, the actual windows and a door, and other finishing touches.

As the weekend nears an end, Wick, Doc, and Harry admire their project.

"Summer is nearly over, Harry," says Wick. "Just look at what we have accomplished."

"Not to mention the money you promised to pay me," adds Harry.

"That we did and we will," assures Doc.

"I could never have done something like this back home," admits Harry.

"If you go back to school and do well at home, you can come back next summer," offers Wick.

"You mean it?" asks Harry.

"You have our word," adds Doc.

"I won't forget that," promises Harry. "When I go home, I'm gonna be proud."

Clangs sound from the nautical channel marker in the distance.

"Harry," says Wick, "I think this island is helping you find your true self."

The next morning, Glenn arrives to take Wick and Doc back to the mainland. He has brought a special delivery letter sent to Wick from New York.

"This arrived yesterday," says Glenn as he hands it to Wick.

Wick opens the letter and has a concerned look on his face. After reading it he hands it to Doc who reads it out loud.

"The court, having received a complaint from the sheriff of Washington County, Maine hereby orders Harold Thompson to return to New York to appear before this court at 10am, August 18th, 1947."

"That's two days from now," exclaims Wick. "For illegal tampering with a lobster trap regulated by Maine state law."

Harry has overhead part of the discussion and comes over.

"What happened?" he asks. "Is there something wrong?"

The clangs from the bell on the nautical channel marker turn menacing.

"We have to take you back to New York with us to appear in court," explains Wick. "Did something happen with a lobster trap?"

"I didn't mean any harm," admits Harry. "But I took a lobster when I was rowing along the coast."

"You stole a lobster?" admonishes Doc.

"I didn't think anyone would see or care. When I went out in the rowboat I bumped into a marker. I remember hearing Mr. Flynn talk about how good they taste."

"It's not that unusual for a teenaged boy to take a lobster," offers Glenn. "If it were up to me, I'd look the other way. For one lobster, it's not like a livelihood is being threatened."

"But it was wrong," Wick tells Harry. "And it could be serious for you because of your situation with the court. You'll have to pack your things and go back with us."

A few minutes later, Harry's duffle bag is packed for the trip to New York. He is momentarily by himself, taking his pigeon cage over toward the water. He removes Dutchman, attaches a tiny canister to the bird's leg, and kisses the bird on the head.

"I know you can make it," Harry says to his Dutchman.

He gives the bird a heave into the air as he whistles. As the bird soars, there is no second whistle and Dutchman flies out of sight. Harry keeps his other bird in the cage and prepares the cage for the return to New York by covering it.

Chapter Nine
The Second Reckoning

Harry sits in a crowded Manhattan Juvenile Court, waiting for his case to be called. He is accompanied by a court-appointed attorney, Thelma, Wick, and Doc.

At that same moment Roseanne is on the roof of her foster parents' apartment building feeding Harry's pigeons as Dutchman lands on top of the pigeon loft. She is in disbelief knowing that Harry took the bird with him to Maine.

"Can't be," Roseanne says to herself. "Could it be? Dutchy, is that you?"

Dutchman coos as it jumps onto Roseanne's hand. She examines the bird's markings and discovers the canister attached to its leg.

"It is you! And what have you brought from Harry?"

Roseanne detaches the canister, pulls out a tightly folded piece of paper, and puts Dutchman in the loft which she has just refreshed with seeds and water. She reads the note to herself.

"Dear sister," she reads. "After your mom died and before Dad left for the war, he asked me to look after you if something happened to him. I'm trying, but I never knew things would be this bad. I know you need to get away from those people. I know you need to see a doctor. I also know when Mom meets you, she will love you right away. My wish is for the three of us to finally be together. We are family. Love, Harry."

Roseanne smiles and there are tears in her eyes as she holds the letter up to her heart.

In Juvenile Court where Harry continues to wait, Judge Wysinger enters the courtroom and ruffles through some papers.

"The court will now hear the case of Harold Thompson," pronounces the judge.

Harry and his attorney come before the judge.

"This court," he proclaims, "received a complaint from the state of Maine that you tampered with a lobster trap that is protected by state law. Did this occur?"

"Yes, sir," says Harry, "but…"

Harry's attorney takes over before Harry can continue. "Your honor, as a first offense in the state of Maine, we are asking that Mr. Thompson pay the appropriate fine and the matter be dismissed. We further appeal that this court be satisfied with that outcome."

Judge Wysinger ruffles through some more papers. "Unfortunately, this court cannot recognize this as a first offense. Your client was in the state of Maine under special permission from this court. He has violated the court's trust."

"Your honor," Harry's attorney replies, "we are pleading for leniency."

"Under the circumstances," the judge responds, "I cannot allow it. Mr. Thompson, you will return to Lavenburg immediately."

The judge gavels. "A court officer will make the appropriate arrangements."

A tearful Thelma hugs Harry, who is stunned as a court officer approaches to escort him away. Wick and Doc have looks of complete helplessness.

That night, Harry is lying on a bed in a stark room at Lavenburg. There is no one to provide any comfort while he fears for his future. He is now hearing voices in his sleep.

"Harry, pay attention," commands a female voice resembling one of his middle school teachers. "If you made a better effort, you wouldn't be a failure at this."

"Harry," says another female voice resembling a former social worker, "we know you're not as smart as some of the others."

"You want to spend the rest of your life in prison?" asks a male voice resembling a former vice principal at his school. "Do you want that, son?"

"When are you joining us?" asks a member of The Dragons. "We got scores to settle."

"You'll never amount to anything," says the voice of another female teacher.

"You better join the Sportsmen soon," says a gang member he encountered. "You never know. You might come home to find your dear mother's throat slit."

Harry is jolted awake in a cold sweat and stares at the ceiling.

Thelma is sitting opposite Harry at the Lavenburg visitation room one week after his incarceration. "You look tired, Harry," says Thelma as she gazes at his face. "Are you able to sleep enough? Are they treating you right?"

"I'm okay and they're keeping me in a room by myself so far. But I have bad dreams and wake up too much. When I wake up, I can't get back to sleep."

"I should talk to them," says Thelma.

"No, don't do that," pleads Harry. "It would probably work against me."

"What can I do to help?" she asks.

"Please keep in touch with the doctors. My time on Dyer Island was the best. I'm so sorry I messed it up."

"Harry, I know you were doing the best you can. And I'm sure the doctors understand that mistakes happen."

"There are too many mistakes," bristles Harry. "If I could change things I would."

"What would you change, dear?" she asks.

"I don't know. Things could be different."

Harry is afraid to bring up his dad's affair and Roseanne. He doesn't want to hurt his mother, so he keeps it inside.

"Never mind," says Harry. "I just want to get through this. The time I spent on the island was the best in my life. The doctors promised I could go back next year. I'm afraid it might not happen because of this."

"It'll happen, Harry. I promise you. It'll happen," Thelma assures him.

Wick and Thelma are seated at a café talking over coffee.

"As far as we're concerned," says Wick. "Harry's time with us on the island was a resounding success. We'd like to have him back next summer."

"Harry would love that," responds Thelma. "He can't stop talking about his experiences there. At least," she sighs, "when I can speak with him."

"Does he have any other close family nearby?" asks Wick.

"No. Well, yes," replies Thelma. "His half-sister Roseanne who is fourteen. But he doesn't know I know about her."

"How can that be?" asks Wick.

"Harry's father was a good man," says Thelma. "But…"
She begins to sob uncontrollably.

"It's okay," says Wick. "You don't have to talk about it."

"I want to talk about it," says Thelma who is re-gaining her composure. "He was a good man. But he had an affair with another woman. She was so young and I couldn't understand it. And she became pregnant and had their daughter. Roseanne was eight when he enlisted to fight in the war. Harry was ten. After he left, Roseanne's mother was killed in a gang fight." Thelma is sobbing once again. "And I'm afraid Roseanne's not very well cared for."

"Who is taking care of her?" asks Wick.

"Foster parents a few blocks away. And they should go to hell! They just want her monthly check. And I feel I can't do anything about it."

Harry is in his room with several books on a table by his bed after visiting Lavenburg's library. The books are opening a new world to him. He is now reading Maugham's *The Razor's Edge*. On the table are other books: Hemingway's *For Whom the Bell Tolls*, Warren's *All the King's Men*, and Orwell's *Animal Farm*.

Later that day, Roseanne is sitting opposite Harry at a table in the visitation room as guards look on.

"It's great to see you, sis," beams Harry.

"I just found out you were here," says Roseanne. "When you didn't come by, I went to your apartment. Your mom answered the door and told me where you were."

"She knows about you?" questions Harry.

Roseanne covers up a lie. "She thinks I'm your girlfriend. I think she likes me."

"That's good," says Harry who seems relieved. "How are my birds?"

"They're doing great. Especially Dutchy!"

"He made it?" Harry asks excitedly.

"Yes. With your letter. It's the most beautiful thing I've ever gotten," she confesses.

"Did you find the money?" asks Harry hopefully. "Did you get to see a doctor?"

"I found the can," replies Roseanne, "but it was empty. I'll be okay."

Roseanne coughs and her breathing becomes more labored as though her mind is now reminded about her illness.

"I gotta go," she says. "I'll visit again next week."

Roseanne rushes out of the room, not giving Harry a chance to follow up.

Chapter Ten
Moving On

F estive balloons and a sign reading "Good Luck, Dr. Jones" hang over the entrance of a Roosevelt Hospital common room where staff and friends have gathered for a send-off party.

Inside, Wick offers a toast.

"We recognize a great surgeon when we see one. Unfortunately, we can't always keep 'em. Wish I could just say 'Doc, please stay!'"

There are chuckles around the room.

"But seriously," continues Wick, "as many of you know, Doc is transferring to the Lahey Clinic in Boston. We all know he'll be taking a part of Roosevelt with him. I raise a glass to wish him the very best of luck."

Glasses clink and there is applause as Doc stands and comes forward while Wick returns to his seat.

"Thanks, Wick, for your kind words. Moving to Boston and working at Lahey, near my old hometown, has been a long-term goal of mine," Doc explains. "But it's not the end of our relationship. As most of you know, Wick and I have invested in an undeveloped island off the coast of Maine where we hope to have adventures."

Wick shouts from his seat. "I hope to put this big Boy Scout to the test!"

There are hearty laughs from around the room.

"And Wick is working on his survival skills," he continues, "but both of us will have to work off those big city habits, like Gus's baked goods."

There are more laughs as Gus's Bakery has become the in-house inspiration for break time at the hospital.

"You are all welcome to visit next summer," Doc adds. "But bring tools!"

"And pastries!" shouts Wick.

There is more laughter and applause as Doc rejoins Wick to mingle with colleagues.

Wick and Doc talk during lunch in the hospital cafeteria.

"Your transfer to Boston shouldn't have any impact on our plans, right?"

"Nope," says Doc. "And I'm getting good feedback in Boston. There are a ton of boys just like Harry who are having difficulties in their adolescence. Broken families, lack of jobs, no hands-on experience with creating things of value. Learning some of the skills we taught Harry could greatly improve the quality of their lives."

"But the other question," poses Wick, "is how can we fund this? I have a lawyer friend who says he can set up a non-profit foundation for us free of charge."

"That could be the answer," responds Doc. "Then we could get support from our communities and that would make it much easier to raise money."

"You know," Wick admits, "this is getting a lot more complicated. We just wanted a vacation spot."

"I guess our altruistic tendencies are getting the best of us," offers Doc. "But it's good. For every Harry out there, there are so many other kids who need help. And, by the way, I can't get Harry's father out of my mind."

Judge Wysinger is in his chambers at his desk looking over a legal brief when his secretary comes on the intercom.

"Judge, you have a call from a police captain James. He says it's about your son, Jerry."

Judge Wysinger answers. "Hello Captain. What can I do for you?"

"I'm afraid it's about your son, Jerry. He was caught with a few other teens painting racist graffiti on the 50th street IRT subway platform."

"Is it serious damage?" asks the judge.

"I'm afraid it's a real mess and will cost significant resources to clean it up. They also removed some of the tiles that were part of the recent renovation of that stop."

The judge puts his hand on his head as he shakes it in exasperation. "Where is he now?"

"We didn't charge him. He's at my office in the Midtown North Precinct on West 54th."

"I'll be down," says the judge, "but give me an hour. And Captain, can you please keep this quiet."

"I'll do my best, your honor."

As Judge Wysinger hangs up the telephone, his intercom chimes in again. "Judge, your last appointment, Dr. Walter Wickson, is here. Shall I send him in?"

"Oh damn," he responds. "Give me a minute and then send him in."

The judge takes a deep breath and then puts his head down on his desk. There is a knock and Wick enters.

"Your honor," says Wick, "I appreciate your taking the time to see me."

"Simply my duty," responds Judge Wysinger. "But I must remind you I cannot discuss Harold Thompson's case with you."

"I understand," says Wick. "And that's not why I'm here. I want to speak with you about a camp for difficult and troubled inner-city teens a colleague and I are forming on an island we've purchased off the coast of Maine."

"Yes?" the judge replies impatiently.

"The island is undeveloped. It doesn't even have electricity or plumbing," replies Wick, "and we want to create a summer work camp to inspire these boys."

"You're going to get these teenaged boys to work? Good luck with that."

"We think we can," assures Wick. "From our initial experiment with Harry Thompson, we believe most troubled boys who are acting out against authority are only responding to the cues society has provided them."

"Interesting," says the judge. "Why are you telling this to me?"

"We want you to keep an open mind," replies Wick. "When it comes to teens who get into trouble, perhaps you can consider our camp as an alternative for some who come before you."

Judge Wysinger is looking at his watch. "I'm sorry, but I've got an important appointment to keep. Please draft a letter about your program and keep me up to date on what you are doing."

"Be happy to," responds Wick, as the judge stands to shake his hand and see him out.

At the Midtown North Precinct House, a. young man is sitting in the corner office of New York City Police Captain James. Jerry Wysinger, age sixteen, is well dressed with perfectly groomed hair and a smirk on his face. He is amusing himself on the captain's desk by carefully stacking a bunch of pens and pencils. His construction project is interrupted as his father, Judge Wysinger, enters with Captain James.

"This time," barks the judge, "you were caught red handed defacing public property. What do you have to say for yourself?"

"I was just having some fun with some friends," Jerry replies. "Didn't hurt anybody. Sorry."

"But somebody has to pay for it," his father scolds. "And it's not the first time. You should have been arrested. Captain James is doing us a favor, but this is the last time, understand?"

"Promise, Dad."

Jerry is thinking to himself. *What is the power of privilege for anyway?*

As Judge Wysinger's only child, Jerry has been brought up in an environment of special treatment, seeing his father sternly enforcing laws with rulings, yet quietly skirting the law when it comes to personal matters. Being above the law for things like today's incident is something Jerry's come to expect.

Christmas decorations adorn the entrance to a large common room at Bellevue Hospital. There is a sign reading, "Welcome back, Dr. Dobson." Inside, the atmosphere is festive with Anne, Wick, and Doc mingling in the crowd. Among those also present is Thelma Thompson. Glasses are clinking as Dr. Richard Simpson, the administrator, summons attention from a podium set up in front of a small stage at the end of the large room.

"As you know…"

The room slowly quiets down.

"As you know," Dr. Simpson says, "Dr. Anne Dobson has been away from us for far too long under very trying circumstances. But the good news is, not only has she defeated tuberculosis, but she's now ready to take on a new challenge by heading up the Trudeau Emphysema Unit at Bellevue."

There is enthusiastic applause as Anne stands and waves.

Harry is all smiles as he leaves Lavenburg with his belongings and Thelma by his side.

"I'm proud of you, Harry," says Thelma. "Your good behavior and use of time means you can now move on with your life."

"Made up all my work at school," beams Harry. "This year is going to be different. Dr. Wickson says I can help plan the next projects for Dyer Island, and I'll be paid for some of the work."

Harry has a new attitude, and it's not because of any programs at Lavenburg. It's his exposure to reading about worlds he's never dreamed of. He was very touched by some of the books he read, especially *Razor's Edge* about a World War I vet who was disillusioned after returning from the war. It's a story he might be deemed too young to read but his real-life experiences make this reading essential. Larry Darnell, the main character, went on a seemingly endless search for transcendent meaning in his life only to finally discover happiness through simplicity.

It's really what I've been doing all along, thinks Harry. *Maybe my life is not as bad as I think.*

But the experiences of Darnell have also given Harry a new respect for his father.

"I'm going to continue to read books," says Harry to Thelma, "And I want to learn more about Dad. They say he was a hero and I want to know more about that."

Thelma is floored that Harry would bring up his father in a new light.

"Your father was a wonderful man," says Thelma as she smiles and experiences an inner feeling of love and gratitude. "I'm glad you want to learn more about him and his service to our country."

Judge Wysinger is at his desk in his court chambers when his secretary interrupts on the intercom.

"Judge, you have a call from police Captain James at the 18th precinct."

The judge picks up the telephone and Captain James is on the other end.

"Judge, I'm sorry to tell you this but it's about your son Jerry again. We just picked him up with another boy. They were joy riding in a stolen car."

There is a shocked look on judge Wysinger's face as he takes a deep breath and swallows. He is a proud man who always has the answers, but now he has no words.

A few days later, Wick is sitting in his stuffed chair reading a newspaper when his telephone rings.

"Doctor Wickson," he answers.

"Hello, Doctor," says the voice on the other end. "This is Judge Thomas Wysinger. I read the material that you sent regarding your camp for boys in Maine. I'd like you to consider taking my son, Jerry, this summer."

Wick does his best not to show signs of excitement.

"We'd be happy to have him, your honor," replies Wick. "But you must realize it will be our second year and life on the island will be, let's say, very rustic."

"Rustic is just what the doctor ordered for Jerry," replies the judge. He nervously clears his throat. "But I'm curious. Will there be other Negro boys at the camp?"

Wick is taken aback by the question but handles it tactfully. "Well, we've never thought about that. Our applications don't ask potential campers about their ethnic or racial backgrounds."

"No matter," acquiesces the judge. "I'd like to send Jerry."

Harry is sitting down to dinner with Thelma in their kitchen. He is nervous because he is about to bring up a subject he never discussed with her before. He's been doing a lot of thinking after having read so many new things in books about the human condition.

"Mom, I need to know…" He stumbles and hesitates in his attempt to choose his words carefully. "Why didn't you tell me about Roseanne?"

Thelma is surprised and unprepared for this. "You know about Dad and Roseanne's mother?" she asks.

"Dad told me before he left for the war," Harry admits. "but he didn't want you to know I knew."

"Oh Harry," Thelma says tearfully. "I would have told you. But. I was upset myself. It hurt so much! And I love you so much! I didn't want to change your view about your father or to upset you."

"But what about Roseanne?" Harry argues with a display of long-delayed anger as he pounds a fist on the table. "It wasn't her fault, and she was left to fend for herself. Now, she's left with those horrible people."

"I know Harry," admits Thelma. "What can we do to make it right?"

Harry stands up and paces around the kitchen table.

"I want Roseanne to see a doctor. She's not well. And the place she lives in is always filled with cigarette smoke and the smell of beer."

"You've been there?"

"Of course I have. You know it's the same building where I keep my pigeons. You've never even come to see the loft I keep them in."

"I guess I've been avoiding things," admits Thelma. "Maybe Wick can help about seeing a doctor."

"And let's figure out a way to bring Roseanne home," demands Harry.

Two weeks later, Anne is in her new clinic at Bellevue Hospital. A plaque on the wall reads "Trudeau Emphysema Center." She is in an examining room finishing with a patient.

"Your x-rays look much improved, Mr. Cornhaber, and if you continue to do better, there is nothing more we need to do now. Just remember, you must not smoke cigarettes, pipes, or cigars with your condition. And avoid smoky rooms."

As Anne moves toward another examining room, she pulls a chart from the wall that has a red rose tucked into it. She smiles as she reads the note that was also tucked in. It is from Wick.

"Dr. Dobson," Anne reads, "I hope your day is going well. How about joining me for dinner Thursday night?"

Anne smiles and remains paused in a pleasant thought before moving on to the next examining room. In the clinic waiting room is Roseanne, seated with Harry.

"Thanks for coming with me," she says to Harry.

"It's okay," he replies. "I don't think it's in your head and I know you can get better."

Anne enters the waiting room and spots the two. "Hello Harry. Is this the young lady I've heard so much about? Come with me, Roseanne, and let's take a look and see what's going on."

Wick and Anne are enjoying a romantic dinner at a cozy restaurant. They are having pre-dinner cocktails. Wick is trying to find a way to express his admiration for her without scaring her off.

"I've been impressed by your enormous way with people and positive influence," says Wick.

"Oh, don't be silly," coos Anne, who is not used to such compliments from men.

"I mean it," insists Wick. "Like what you've done for Doc. Because of your direct honesty, he has entirely stopped smoking."

"Well, that's just about healthy living," Anne reasons. "Doc understands what's healthy and not. He just needed a nudge."

"And then there's me," replies Wick who wants the conversation to move in a slightly different direction. "I've got to admit…"

He pauses while he searches for the right words.

"I've got to admit…"

"Yes?" asks Anne as Wick pauses and stumbles again.

"I simply don't want to see any other women."

"Wanna know a secret?" Anne asks coyly.

Wick nods.

"I feel the same way."

They smile as they gaze into each other's eyes as if a burden had been lifted. They hold hands across the table.

Three weeks later, Roseanne's foster parents are sitting with Roseanne in New York Family Court in Manhattan, where a judge will announce a decision on Roseanne's custody. Seated behind them are Harry and Thelma with their attorney. Wick and Anne are seated in the gallery.

"This should be an easy case for the judge," says Wick to Anne.

"You would think so," says Anne. "My diagnosis for Roseanne is based on solid medical practice."

"It was smart for you to urge Thelma to petition family court to examine Roseanne's living conditions," replies Wick

Judge William Murdock gavels the court to order.

"I will now issue my ruling on the petition regarding custody of minor Roseanne Hernandez," the judge pronounces. "It has come to the court's attention that Miss Hernandez has been diagnosed with chronic bronchitis and there is a finding that the living conditions provided by foster parents Ely and Susan Jones are aggravating that condition. The Joneses have testified they cannot provide Miss Hernandez with a smoke-free environment. Therefore, I am ruling that Miss Hernandez be removed from the Joneses' custody and the court will entertain the petition that Mrs. Thelma Thompson be awarded temporary custody. It is so ruled."

As the judge gavels for the next case, the Joneses depart quickly with Roseanne turning away and refusing to speak with them. Thelma, Harry, and Roseanne huddle together sharing hugs while they are congratulated by Anne and Wick. They are all smiles as they depart together.

Chapter Eleven
New Beginnings

Older Harry continues to walk with his cane on a Dyer Island path as he tells the Camp Dyer story to Johnny along with elderly Wick. Johnny is beginning take an interest because hearing about Harry at age 15 and the stories surrounding his young life mirrors his circumstances and emotions.

"Camp Dyer started that first year with only ten boys," says Harry. "They were recruited from the New York City and Boston areas and it was free for them to attend. They were provided everything they needed for the summer and were taught trades while working on projects as part of a community away from home.

"Did they still have Glenn and his boat to take them back and forth?" asks Johnny who seems to be taking more interest.

"No," replies Wick. "While Glenn was still involved with us, we thought all those back- and-forth trips were too much to ask from him. So, we were able to purchase a retired Boston police boat with the help of a bank loan."

"Camp life wasn't easy," adds Harry. "Everything that arrived on the island had to be carried by hand. There was no pier, no road from the fisherman's shack to the northeast cove. There was no tractor, no cement mixer, no power tools, and no electricity for that matter. The boys worked together with hand tools and the help of able-bodied men experienced in the building trades who volunteered their time."

Johnny is beginning to realize the enormity of the effort to make Camp Dyer a reality. "How were you and Doc able to spend so much time away from your work at home?" he asks.

"It wasn't easy," replies Wick. "But we thought the work with the boys was so important we used all our weekends and vacation time to be on the island."

"What were they able to do?" asks Johnny.

"The first goal was to build a pier at the cove," says Harry, "and then the lodge which today is the second largest building on the island. The lodge would provide permanent shelter and a base for all activities. The ten campers also paired up to plan and choose sites for additional small cabins which they would begin building on weekends. The cabins would be finished the following year as each of the boys were invited back. They chose names for their cabins which would eventually be occupied by later generations of boys."

It's the first year at Camp Dyer. The ten boys include Harry and Jerry who are now sixteen. Charlie Huffman, another sixteen-year-old, appears to be the largest and strongest among them all. The other seven are all fifteen except for David, who is fourteen and was allowed to attend because of very difficult circumstances at home. Wick and Doc are joined by Bill Withers, a building contractor and Boy Scout leader from Boston who has volunteered to help get the early construction projects going. The boys display great attitudes and are supportive of one another. Jerry, however, exudes an air of superiority. Harry is aware Jerry is the son of the judge who sent him to Lavenburg, but Jerry does not know about Harry's circumstances.

"Why are you here?" Jerry asks Harry.

"I'm here because I wanted to come back," replies Harry. "The doctors brought me here last summer and I helped build the cabin near the spot where the lodge will be built."

"You don't mind the work?" asks Jerry.

"No, because I've learned so much and I've gotten stronger."

"Don't care for the work," says Jerry. "I'm here because my dad told me I had to be, and I plan to do as little as possible."

Harry offers no response. He is overthinking now about how he should interact with Jerry.

Building supplies and tools are brought in on a small barge that is moored at the dock by the fisherman's shack. The first order of business is to expand the temporary camp that Wick, Doc, and Harry used the previous summer. Two fifteen-foot square platforms are constructed for two large tents that are each designed to sleep six people. This will be the boys' permanent living quarters for the summer. Each boy is assigned an army cot to sleep on. Wick, Doc, and Bill use the fisherman's shack as their sleeping quarters.

"We need to build an outhouse," announces Wick. "I need a couple volunteers to dig a ditch for it."

Two of the boys agree and go to work.

"We need a volunteer to be our camp cook," announced Doc. Jimmy Cooke raises his hand.

"My name is Cooke," he says, "and I love to cook."

"You're in," says Doc, as there is laughter among the boys.

The boys agree that they will all pitch in to help Jimmy when needed. The next morning, a makeshift kitchen with army surplus utensils is in working order with Jimmy producing pancakes, boxes of breakfast cereals, eggs, coffee, and coffee cake at Doc's requestd. They are happy campers.

"We will need a better place to eat our meals," says Doc. "Who can help design and build a platform with attached benches that will be big enough for all of us to sit?"

Two boys raise their hands, Bill Withers pitches them a design, and they begin to work.

By the end of day three at Camp Dyer, they had built platforms, put up tents, created an outhouse ready for use, put a makeshift kitchen into service, and built a large picnic table.

On day four, they cleared a wide path from the camp at the fisherman's shack to the new building sites at the cove. The boys form a convoy to transport tools and building materials from the barge to be stored at the cabin built by Wick, Doc, and Harry the previous year. In the interest of equal treatment for all, no one occupies the cabin for sleeping. Then the boys take to the woods to seek out appropriate trees to be cut and fashioned into logs for the new pier and a lodge. The lodge will be large enough to house all the campers. Harry and Wick take charge, instructing the boys on how to cut and spud the trees to be stacked for drying.

The next project is setting the boundaries for the lodge's foundation. After Bill and Doc supervise staking and measuring, Bill instructs Harry and Charlie on how to dig trenches for the footings.

"Way to go, Charlie," says Harry as they begin. We're going to make a good team."

The footings, ten in all, are one foot wide and, because of the frost line, need to be three feet deep. Fortunately, the ground is mostly soil with a few rocks. Four of the other boys are sent to a sandy part of the shore about one hundred yards from the construction site. They have named it the beach because of its lack of rocks and high sand content. The boys make a stretcher out of poles and a four by eight sheet of plywood to haul piles of sand and stones gathered along the shore back to the site. They also carry sea water in buckets that will be used to mix concrete in a large tub.

As each hole is completed, a wooden mold is sunk to the bottom. There are two molds that will be re-used five times each. After a mold is in place, a mixture of concrete and stones is poured in over five-foot sections of steel rebar placed in the molds. Once the concrete in each footing cures, the mold is removed and placed into another ditch. Bill decides that each footing must stand two feet above the surface. That would allow for a crawl space under the lodge. It takes a couple days for each footing to set before the mold is pulled out and re-used. It's a slow process but, meanwhile, the cutting and spudding of trees continues until a good stack of logs, about twenty feet long, are accumulated. After twelve days the footings are complete.

The boys take lots of breaks and go back to the camp for lunches and snacks prepared by Jimmy. Jimmy sometimes rotates his job with another boy. But the boys decide they want Jimmy to be the permanent cook and they get no argument from him. During this time, Doc begins to assign regular responsibilities for a few of the boys. Billy, a fifteen-year-old experienced in handling power boats, is put in charge of managing and maintaining the police boat shuttling to and from Wyman's Landing for a wide variety of purposes.

After the third day at camp, nearly all the boys, except for big Charlie, were complaining of aches and pains all over their bodies as every muscle was exercised to the limit, over and over again. But after a week or so, there are no more complaints as everyone, perhaps with the exception of Jerry, is getting stronger. At one point, as if to demonstrate his strength, Charlie puts seventy pound bags of cement under each arm while carrying a five gallon can of water about a hundred yards to the construction site. The boys jokingly call him "Charlie the hulk," and he enjoys it.

This work is also considered play by most of these boys, many who have struggled to find their identities in their home environments. They are given adult-sized jobs that their peers come to rely on. That usually results in adult-sized efforts on the parts of most of the boys. But the work fuels extreme appetites. Doc makes sure there is plenty of food to go around. He spent the summer months reaching out to food distributers asking for donations of non-perishable canned and dried foods and, when possible, foods that had a shorter shelf-life. A typical breakfast might be a whole box of cereal, or a plate of four to six eggs with bacon, plus fruits and juices. Kool-Aide is also a staple. Lunches are somewhat lighter, but dinners again are very large meals heavy on carbohydrates.

The boys are working on the foundation for the lodge, laying down logs that have been sawed flat on two sides to be placed onto the footings for the bottom course of the walls. It's heavy work and requires a team effort. Jerry is not taking part in the lifting while acting like the boss. Harry is working with the newer boys lifting a heavy log into place.

"You guys are weaklings," pronounces Jerry.

"You're much bigger than us," says David, the fourteen-year-old who is one of the smallest boys. "Why aren't you lifting with us?"

"David's right," says Harry, "so give us a hand."

"You think you have the right to order me around?" says Jerry, taking issue with Harry's request.

Harry and the boys put down the log they are lifting while the dispute is settled. Harry confronts Jerry directly.

"Since I have more experience here, I have a responsibility to lead and make sure we all pitch in together," he asserts.

Jerry's reaction is to give Harry a hard shove backward, nearly knocking him to the ground.

"Where I come from," claims Jerry, "I don't take orders from people like you."

Harry pushes back even harder, causing Jerry to fall backwards and onto his back.

"You are now in the Camp Dyer community," says Harry firmly. "You either do the work with us or I report you."

Harry is surprised at himself for being able to stand up to Jerry so decisively. And it works. Jerry is not used to others standing up to him and shuts up. He silently joins the others in lifting. They manage to get the first heavy log into place. Then another, and another.

The camp environment straightens Jerry out pretty quickly, as none of the boys are having any part of his authoritarian posturing. There are no more incidents. At the end of each day the boys, and even Jerry, take pride in the progress they are making.

At the pier site, the boys focus on bringing heavy logs onto a barge for the short trip to a cage being built up in the water from the bottom by fastening logs together with rebar to support a pier. The new logs are lifted to the top of the cage, later filled with heavy rocks. Pressure treated planks are then laid down for the walkway on top. When the new pier is finished, the old police boat can bring new building materials directly to the lodge worksite.

The building of the lodge is much more complicated.

The lodge is now taking shape as more logs are put in place above the foundation. Walls go up. After they are in place, they lay boards on the rafters. The boys string a web of heavy ropes across to balance themselves precariously while they nail the boards in place.

"When will the first of you fall?" quips Bill.

The boys pay no attention and continue as they are until one of them slips and falls onto the floor below. Fortunately, he is not hurt, laughs it off with the other boys, jumps back up, and continues.

A frame for the roof is taking shape. The boys lay boarding for the roof, then climb on top to cut off the uneven ends with a hand saw. This requires balancing on the edge of the roof. Among them is Charlie who all of a sudden disappears from his post. The very next moment, he is climbing a ladder back onto the roof and continues where he left off. Charlie had taken a tumble off the roof onto a pile of dirt fifteen feet below but is no worse for the wear.

Also built into the design of the lodge is a large fireplace, which will contain a large steel heatilator to conserve and distribute heat from the fire. Getting the heatilator to the island is the most difficult lifting project the boys undertake. With the help of a crane at Wyman's Landing, the heatilator is lowered into the barge and towed to the island.

"How are we going to move that off the barge?" Harry wonders aloud.

"The difficult we do at once," says Charlie borrowing a phrase from the camp motto. "But this is definitely going to take longer."

"How do you think the ancient Egyptians moved the stones for the pyramids?" poses Doc.

The boys have little time to mull over solving that problem and employ their spontaneous, collective ingenuity. Once the heavy steel stove arrives on the barge, it is grounded near the beach. At low tide, the boys place a series of logs up the beach toward the construction site. Under pressure to finish the job before the new tide comes in, eight boys, four on each side, manage to lift it off the barge and roll it onto the logs which act as sort of a wheel. Finally, the boys manage to roll the steel hulk onto smaller and longer logs that they lift, four on each side, like pallbearers. Finally, getting the heatilator into place in the fireplace requires nothing short of collective brute force. Once in place, the stonework around the fireplace can be completed.

Finally, the boys are on top laying roofing shingles with the help of Wick and Bill.

While finishing touches to the lodge continue, Doc spends time visiting the Washington County seat on the mainland to meet selectmen. Doc wants to make sure the town officials understand the goal at Camp Dyer is an effort to teach teenage boys about the value of work and to gain skills to move their personal lives in the right direction. *It is important*, thinks Doc, *to persuade the county elders that Camp Dyer deserves its tax-free status.*

It is a very satisfying moment when the boys move their belongings from the tents by the Fisherman's shack to their new home in the lodge. The large fireplace creates a comfortable spot to assemble as August evenings are getting cooler.

Anne spends as many weekends as she can from her busy schedule at Bellevue Hospital visiting Wick and viewing the progress on the island. During a break from the work, Wick and Anne take a walk alone together in a remote section of the woods toward the other side of the island. Anne stops frequently to study the small plants growing on the woodland floor.

"This is remarkable," beams Anne. "It's pristine. I've never seen so many kinds of native ferns, mosses, and flowers."

Anne whirls up and around from her crouch to give Wick a big hug. They hold hands as they emerge from the woods into a large opening overlooking the Northeast coast. They are now looking over a field of wild blueberries.

"The birds are picking the blueberries!" proclaims Anne. "Can we eat them too?"

Wick bends down to pick some berries from one of the plants, eats a few, and places the rest in Anne's hand.

"You'll never taste a sweeter blueberry than the tiny ones growing wild here in Maine."

Anne puts them in her mouth and smiles. They begin working their way down the hill, picking and eating along with the birds and the butterflies. Musical clangs like wind chimes can be heard from the bell on a nautical channel marker in the distance. They share a long, drawn-out kiss. The two seem like they are one with the natural wonders around them. They spot rabbits, then dragonflies, then a fleeting fox.

At a cabin worksite, Harry and Jerry install roofing shingles on a small, newly built cabin not far from the lodge. Jerry is thinking to himself how his life at home is so different from Harry's. He thinks about how he acted when he first arrived at camp, how Harry stood up to him, and why he is glad he did.

"Once you've done one roof," says Harry, "the others are all the same."

"Kind of like learning to ride a bike," says Jerry in agreement. "You have a bike at home?"

"Wish I did," responds Harry. "We couldn't afford one." Harry pauses. "I guess I don't even know how to ride," he adds.

"I forgot," says Jerry. "You're from…" He stops himself to change his tack. "You know something?" he asks. "Privilege is not what it's cracked up to be."

"How's that?" asks Harry.

"I've got everything I want. But I don't feel good about it. In fact, I feel a bit guilty about being a judge's son. I think you're making something out of your life. And I guess I've learned something this summer."

The clangs from the bell on the nautical channel marker in the bay below seem to indicate a special moment for the friends.

"When we get back to New York," asks Jerry, "want to learn to ride my bike?"

"That would be swell!" beams Harry.

At the end of that first camp year, families and friends of each boy are invited to a lobster banquet to celebrate the culmination of the first camp year. The lobsters are provided by Glenn, who also takes everyone on a boat tour around the island. As for the campers, they are given awards and invited to brag about their accomplishments. They also decide on ways to be better organized for next year's projects. They would be divided into work groups, they decide. There will be a boat crew to run the shuttle to and from the mainland. There would also be crews for plumbing and other construction. Finally, the boys decide there should be a boy director to be elected for each coming year based on his leadership qualities.

In a keynote following the dinner, Doc offers congratulations to the boys who made the year a success.

"You should all be proud of what we have accomplished together this summer," says Doc. "Each and every one of you played an important role. We are living proof of our camp motto: The difficult we do at once. The impossible takes a little longer."

The boys stand and cheer and recite the motto together. As the chant subsides, Doc continues. "And now, here is the result of your vote for our first boy director for next season. The vote is unanimous for Harry Thompson."

There are cheers and hoots as Harry stands up, blushing in pride. Later, at high tide, the boys give Harry a surprise celebratory heave from the pier into the water. Everyone laughs and cheers, including Harry.

Chapter Twelve
The Seed

With the first camp summer a fond memory, it's Sunday in early fall as Anne and Wick sit for brunch at their favorite New York City café.

"I already miss the island," confesses Anne.

"It was special," agrees Wick. "It seems like those weekends went by in a flash."

"Can't wait for next summer," says Anne.

"You know, the boys really like you," offers Wick.

"You think so? I can't imagine why. The first thing I notice is a rash or if they have a cut or bruise or something out of place."

"Maybe that's it," says Wick. "They need some mothering. And I think they like it. You will make a great mother."

"Only with the right man," says Anne with a playful smile.

It's a winter day as Doc, now living in Massachusetts, walks into a YMCA in a rough area of South Boston. He speaks to a small group of teenaged boys who have gathered in the gym as part of a weight-lifting program run by the city.

"How many of you have plans to go to college?" Doc asks.

No one raises a hand.

"How many of you have summer plans?"

Mark raises his hand. He's a fifteen-year-old wearing a t-shirt with a pack of cigarettes folded into its left sleeve. He's a wannabe grownup with an air of toughness.

"What's your name?" asks Doc.

"My friends call me Southy," he says as some of the others come out with a chuckle.

"I'm gonna learn to work the streets," he says with a strong Boston accent. "I shoot craps and I'm good at it."

"Craps huh," replies Doc. "Where will that get you?"

"I figure I can make a few bucks," Southy comes back.

Doc asks the question again. "But where will that GET you?"

Southy shrugs his shoulders and doesn't have a comeback.

"I'm a medical doctor at Lahey Clinic," says Doc. "But I also own a small island off the coast of Maine and run a summer camp designed for boys just like you."

"A summer camp!" exclaims one of the boys. "That's for sissies. What's in it for us?"

"No sissies at our camp," says Doc. "We build things that strong, grown men build. What if I told you we could teach you to be a carpenter, a plumber, a boat pilot, and a community leader all in one summer?"

At Doc's house in suburban Boston, Fred, a boy who just turned sixteen, is fixing a gutter on Doc's roof. He wears a carpenter's belt. When the job is done, he folds the ladder, puts it in the garage, and heads inside where Doc is making lunch. Fred sits down at the kitchen table as Doc brings some sandwiches and sits down with him.

"Gutter's fixed," says Fred, "but we might need some new fasteners."

"Good you noticed," replies Doc. "We'll pay a visit to the hardware store."

While Doc is a surgeon at Lahey clinic he's been on the lookout for boys who might be deserving candidates for Camp Dyer's second summer. Fred is from a broken home in South Boston and has moved in with Doc while he works odd jobs and learns skills that will be helpful for the island.

Meantime, Wick and Anne have made lifechanging plans on their future together. Wick has asked Anne to marry him.

It's a spring day at a church in Rahway, New Jersey as a crowd waits outside the church's front doors. Suddenly the doors burst open as Wick and Anne emerge as husband and wife in a shower of confetti and rice.

Later, at a nearby catering hall, groups of people linger outside smoking cigarettes. Signs on the hall entrance read "No Smoking" and "Smoke Free Wedding." Inside, Anne and Wick are making the rounds at their reception. Anne gives Harry a kiss on the cheek and he blushes as Thelma and Roseanne look on. Jerry and several of the boys from Camp Dyer are also there as well as Glenn, his wife, and his fourteen-year-old son.

"Glenn, we are so happy you could come!" beams Anne. She whispers in his ear. "I hope you don't mind the no smoking rule."

"Oh no," Glenn proudly responds. "Didn't ya' know? I quit." Glenn turns to his wife and son. "This is my wife Jeanne and our son Glenn Jr."

"Pleased to meet you both," says Anne. "Glenn, you really quit smoking?"

"You sent me a powerful message and I'm grateful," he responds.

"And I can't thank you enough," says Jeanne. "Since Glenn has stopped, he no longer keeps me up at night with his snoring and coughing."

They all laugh as their conversation is interrupted by the clinking of glasses. Anne and Wick return to their seats at the head table while Doc, the best man, proposes a toast.

"When I first met Wick, I had just gotten out of the service at the end of the war. While I was technically his supervisor at Roosevelt, he is the one I credit for my success as a surgical fellow. Not only did

Wick's up-to-date medical knowledge save my butt, but his advanced technique in finding the right spots for a cat nap was the real clincher."

There are hearty laughs at Doc's joke.

"And then there's Anne. She's not just another smart and pretty lady but she's got real magic. I had never seen Wick disappear so often until after they met."

There is more laughter.

"But there's much more to Anne," Doc continues. "Her lectures on the dangers of polluted air have won over many minds and even persuaded me recently to give up cigarettes entirely. But she also had to overcome a diagnosis of tuberculosis that many have not survived. And now, she's turning her recovery into a new milestone in her career." Doc raises his glass. "Please join me in wishing Anne and Wick a long and happy life together."

There are cheers and "hear hears" as Doc rejoins the couple at the table. The band strikes up the Frankie Laine hit song "All of Me" as everyone gets up to join Anne and Wick on the dance floor.

Doc is on the telephone at his office at Lahey Clinic in Burlington, Massachusetts.

"Thank you, Major Wilson, for returning my call. As I mentioned in my message, I've been trying to find the identity of the African American soldier who saved my life while I was a medic treating a comrade of his in Burma. I think that soldier might have been Corporal Harold S. Thompson who was a tank gunner deployed there. He was later killed in action and awarded the Distinguished Service Cross. Have you been able to trace him yet?"

"We've been checking," replies Major Wilson, "and it remains a possibility. But the records are incomplete, and the Army cannot say it with certainty. I'll be happy to let you know if I should receive further information."

"I appreciate your efforts, Major," replies Doc.

Chapter Thirteen
The Greening

It's early in the morning before dawn in late June at Wick and Anne's apartment. Wick is still sleeping, and Anne is whispering into his ear. "Honey? Wick? Wick, honey?"

Anne turns on the light and Wick's eyes pop open.

"Time to go to camp," exclaims Anne.

Soon, the woody station wagon is on the road for the eight-hour drive from New York to Maine. The wagon is cramped with supplies for Camp Dyer and the theme from "Rawhide" plays on the car radio.

"That's a good soundtrack for our adventure," offers Wick. "Feel like a pioneer?"

"I suppose," replies Anne. "It will be a new adventure with ten additional boys," reasons Anne.

"Twenty boys will be more of a challenge, for sure. It will also allow us to accomplish much more this season," says Wick.

Later, the woody wagon arrives in Milbridge and pulls into the parking lot where Glenn along with his son Glenn Jr., are waiting for them. Wick notices the police boat is not in its slip at the pier.

"Good," says Wick. "The shuttle is gone and that means Doc and Bill have already arrived."

Glenn waves as Wick calls out.

"Hello Glenn! How's the fishing?"

"Can't complain," Glenn shouts back.

After more greetings, the four begin to move the contents of the wagon over to Glenn's boat. There are medical supplies, procured from the hospital. Blankets, pillows, and sheets are carried in black pliofilm bags. There are also large, aluminum cooking utensils packed into burlap gunnysacks, extra batteries for flashlights, and hand tools for a variety of work.

As Glenn's boat arrives at Camp Dyer's new pier, Doc and his friends are there to greet them.

"The pier is still standing!" shouts Wick.

"Strong as a castle," replies Doc.

Anne and Wick head up the gangplank and greet Doc with hugs.

"You made good time from Boston," says Wick. "Looks like the old police boat weathered the winter well."

"Like a battleship. Fired up right away," responds Doc who turns to the men who are with him.

"This is Bill Lathrup and George Bussell, old friends and former scout leaders from Boston. And you already know Bill Withers"

Wick shakes their hands. "Glad you could join us this summer, and glad you're back Bill."

Wick notices the black Newfoundland dog with Doc.

"You brought Inky?"

"Yep," says Doc. "He's now an honorary boy."

There are hearty laughs as they begin to unload Glenn's boat, which includes canned food supplies loaded earlier. They are all carried to the lodge. Next to the lodge, two large tents have been erected.

"Where'd you get the tents?" asks Wick.

"A donation from the Boston police," replies Doc, "along with a bunch of other things the Army sent them. The tents each sleep eight, so we should be in good shape for shelter."

A school bus filled with campers arrives at the pier parking lot in Milbridge. There are cheers from the boys inside as the long trip is ending. Soon, a steady stream of boys with their personal baggage is moving up the gangplank as the shuttle brings them across the sound. Most are carrying their gear in gunny sacks and canvas duffle bags. Among them are Harry and Jerry Wysinger. Harry spots Wick and Doc.

"Hello doctors. You remember Jerry?"

"We sure do," replies Wick. "Welcome back, Jerry. You and Jerry can move your things directly into your cabin. You know it needs finishing touches, but you will both manage that."

"Yes sir," replies Harry.

There are more familiar faces and some new ones arriving, like Mark and Julio who display all the trappings of city street kids, not dressed for the island work environment.

"I'd like you to meet Mark McGuire from South Boston and Julio Perez from the Bronx, New York," says Doc.

"My friends call me Southy," says Mark. "It's kinda my territory."

Southy is one of the boys Doc met at the YMCA. He is dressed in jeans rolled up slightly to above the ankles with white socks and penny loafers and a short-sleeved plaid shirt over a white t-shirt with sleeves rolled up as far as possible. His hair is slicked back and he carries a big comb in his back pocket.

Julio is dressed in plaid pants, a white t-shirt, and high top basketball sneakers over black socks. His natty hair is covered with a white sailor's cap and he sports a gold chain with a cross around his neck. "You can just call me Julio. That sounds like who-Leo."

The four laugh it up as if to make fun of their contrasting looks.

As more boys arrive for that second summer of camp there is a lot of excitement and anticipation as they settle into assigned spots in tents or the lodge. But it isn't long before they become immersed in learning how to manage their work in this very different environment.

The boys learn to use tools like axes, saws, and a spudding tool for the job they'll have harvesting more trees from the forest for lumber. Missteps abound as the new boys are city kids with no woodland skills.

Southy, for example, is swinging an axe at a small tree with the blunt end doing the impact hoping the mere force of the blow will do the damage. Harry teaches him to use the sharp end to angle a notch. Julio then pushes on the tree thinking the notch itself will do the trick. He is shown to angle the axe on the other side of the tree slightly above the first notch to finish the job. There are cheers when the tree falls.

The fact that the senior boys can do most of the instruction with adult supervisors staying in the background seems to be an approach that not only empowers the experienced boys but provides encouragement to the new ones.

Anne stocks the lodge infirmary while providing an orientation for Louise, the newly hired camp nurse. She's from New York City where she works at an all-girls' academy during the school months. She volunteered to work at the camp for a small fraction of her real salary because of the mere adventure of the opportunity. She has also brought along Pie, her pet Newfoundland dog.

"When I mentioned Pie to Doc," says Louise, "he insisted I bring him. He and Inky now are the best of friends, with the run of the island."

It isn't long before the boys are working along with adult supervisors to build the foundation of a much larger building in a nearby clearing. It will be thirty by seventy feet and become the mess hall and meeting place. A sign is put up reading, "The difficult we do at once, the impossible takes longer." The building of the mess hall is the key focus of the summer, along with some additional small cabins which the boys are allowed to work on only during the weekends.

The boys experience occasional accidents, but their injuries are mostly minor and only require a short visit to the infirmary. Sometimes, Wick or Doc are summoned to provide the expertise of a physician. With scrapes or muscle sprains and strains, which often occurred to ankles or wrists, Doc's favorite therapy is to have the boy spend fifteen minutes soaking in cold saltwater on the bank off the cove near the lodge. In summer, the water is always a chilly fifty-five degrees and contains all the therapeutic minerals that seem to do the job. More severe injuries might result in a trip to a clinic in Milbridge or Ellsworth. Doc is also known to take advantage of his experience with hypnosis as a form of controlling and treating pain.

Doc learned hypnosis from Chinese physicians he met during his time in the service and kept data on his use of it as a surgeon. He observed that patients bled less, had fewer complications, and recovered faster when he took the time to speak to them using his calming voice and reassurance encouraging them to relax, trust him, and not even think about the operation. That was his experience in over ten thousand gall bladder operations he performed.

One of the Dyer boys was out cutting firewood. He swung an axe for a final cut, causing the axe to glance off to the side and cut the big toe on his right foot. He was hobbling in pain when he made it to the infirmary where Doc was waiting for him. Doc, speaking to him in a calm and soothing voice, gave him a shot of morphine and said it would take effect nearly immediately, even knowing it would actually take at least twenty minutes. The boy was very receptive to hypnosis and the pain went away immediately after Doc touched his shoulder and put him in a deep hypnotic state. Doc cleaned the wound, sutured it, and bandaged it in fifteen minutes. Two days later, the bandages are removed, and the boy is back at work as though it never happened.

Chilly evenings are often spent in front of a roaring fire at the lodge as Doc tells stories from his experiences in the war. The boys sit comfortably on cushions. Among them is Binocs, the youngest, playfully called that by the boys because of his habit of carrying binoculars wherever he goes. The German binoculars with expensive Carl Zeiss lenses had been acquired by his father in the war. Binocs had promised his dad to never let them out of his sight. Tonight, Doc is teaching the boys about hypnosis and Binocs is the perfect candidate for being put in a hypnotic state.

"Your eyes are getting heavy," says Doc in a calm and soothing voice. "Your arms are relaxed and beginning to weigh on you. Your legs, your toes, and stomach are all relaxing."

"My eyes were closed, and I could only hear Doc's voice," Binocs later recalls.

After a few moments, Doc lights a match and heats the end of a safety pin until it glows deep red.

"Now I'm going to prove you are in a deep hypnotic state," says Doc.

After letting the safety pin cool for a few seconds Doc pinches the skin on Binocs' wrist, shoves the pin through the two layers of skin and closes the pin.

"Do you feel anything?" asks Doc.

"Nope, I feel nothing," says Binocs.

"Now we're going to do an experiment," Doc says. "At my command, your spirit will leave your body and sit on the mantel above the fire."

"Yes," replies Binocs. "I am sitting on the edge of the mantel."

"Can you see three boys sitting on the cushion below?" asks Doc.

"Yes, I see them," replies Binocs while his eyes remain closed.

Before the exercise, Doc had asked the three other boys to assume a certain position with certain facial expressions when he prompted them. With the boys following Doc's cue, he continues to speak to Binocs while in his deep trance.

"Without opening your eyes, describe exactly what the boys are doing," prompts Doc.

"Yes," says Binocs, "I see Joe on the left with his legs crossed, I see Jim in the middle sitting straight with his head tilted to the side, and Sam crouching down like a lion with a snarl on his face."

Binocs, without opening his eyes, describes the boys' positions exactly as they are.

"You will now rejoin the boys," commands Doc.

He brings Binocs back fully awake with a snap of his finger and the four boys have a great laugh.

"The experience was so real," Binocs later recalls. "It is so vivid, so real to me just as if it occurred yesterday."

Binocs later became a Camp Dyer senior counselor, an adult supervisor, and a true believer in the power of hypnosis.

On Sundays, Wick and Doc insist the boys clean up and go to the Methodist Church in Milbridge. The church is interdenominational so each boy's religious faith, if they have one, is honored.

"There's great history in this church," Doc tells the boys. "It can be traced back to the Seaman's Friend Society in Boston when floating mariner's churches were created."

"Churches on ships?" Southy asks.

"Yes," says Doc. "The pastor and choir would travel to ships anchored in the area and present a service after boarding. They brought musical instruments with them and, besides preaching the gospel, provided welcomed entertainment for the men. There was great concern during those times over conditions on what many called hell ships, when sailors were kept at sea for as long as a year under poor conditions. Many became alcoholics which might explain why some of those musical sermons got a bit out of hand."

Doc, the consummate storyteller, often stretched history a bit in favor of telling a good story.

"In this church," Doc continues, "the spirit of mariners from the past are ever present."

The boys are welcomed warmly by the small congregation at Milbridge Methodist. After services, they always look forward to attending a social hour with snacks and sweets like ice cream.

As the work on the mess hall resumes, for the first time on the island there is a serious accident involving the use of one of the new power tools. The Lombard Company had donated a new cast aluminum chain saw. It's one of the first chain saws to be powered by gasoline and is light enough to be operated by one person.

As a more experienced camper, Harry is using the chain saw to cut a large tree that had already been notched so it would fall in a predicted direction. Several other boys and Doc watch as the tree comes down. But as it is falling, it kicks upward causing the saw to kick back into Harry, cutting him in the neck. As Harry falls back, the base of the newly cut tree lands on Harry's left leg. Doc and the boys rush to his aid.

"Harry, did you get cut?" Doc asks.

But the answer quickly becomes obvious.

"I think so," says Harry. "And my leg, I can't move it and it hurts real bad."

There is a gash in his neck and Harry's leg is trapped awkwardly under the fallen tree.

"Get Wick and someone from the infirmary right away," Wick shouts to one of the boys.

Doc grabs a towel from his backpack. He rips part of it off to make a bandage and examines Harry where he lies on the ground. He then wraps it around Harry's neck wound and puts pressure on the wound area as he shouts to the other boys.

"The tree! We've got to pry the tree off Harry's leg."

Two boys use two by six boards to pry the tree up but with no success until Charlie, back for his second year, uses his enormous strength to pry it up. As Wick arrives with Louise, he and Doc pull Harry back from under the tree as it is lifted.

"My leg hurts," cries Harry in anguish, "and I can't move it."

"Don't try to move it," says Wick. "We're going to carry you over to the infirmary."

Wick and Doc put their medical training to use to lift Harry onto the stretcher. "One, two, three,.." And they lift Harry in a single movement onto the two-man stretcher which has been placed on the ground next to him.

"Go tell the boys at the dock to get the boat ready," shouts Wick to another one of the boys. "We're taking Harry to Ellsworth."

Doc speaks to Harry in a calm and soothing voice.

"Harry, you're going to be ok."

As Harry is moved from the police boat, into an ambulance for the thirty-minute ride to Ellsworth General Hospital, Doc stays with him and uses his hypnotic skills to keep Harry calm and focused on positive thoughts.

Later, Wick and Doc, both in hospital scrubs, are assisting an emergency room physician who is examining Harry.

"He is lucky," says the ER doctor. "It just missed the artery and major vessels but it's a ragged cut."

He whispers to Wick and Doc who nod in agreement.

"A half an inch more and he would have bled out."

He raises his voice to address Harry directly.

"We're going to do some stitches, so you won't have a big scar. As far as your leg, it's a compound fracture."

"Are you in pain?" Wick asks.

"Yeah, it hurts pretty bad," responds Harry weakly.

"We're giving you something for the pain," says the ER doctor who is administering a drip line into a vein in Harry's left arm, "while we re-set those bones."

"You're in good hands Harry," adds Wick. "You're going to be fine."

"Will I be able to go back to camp?" asks Harry.

"We'll see," answers Doc, even though it is clear to him there is little chance.

"We're keeping you here tonight," adds Doc. "I'll stay over with you."

Later, in the hospital cafeteria, Wick and Doc are having coffee and a sandwich. "Remember?" asks Wick. "This was my worst fear."

"Yes," admits Doc. "We're going to have to be more careful in supervising the boys with these tools. It was smart to hire Louise for the infirmary, but it doesn't help much with an accident like Harry's."

"It's disappointing we have to send Harry home," says Wick. "It'll be a real blow to him after what he has achieved."

"He was at the top of the world," adds Doc, "and becoming a real leader. I've never seen him so confident."

Three weeks later, Harry is laid up on a couch at his New York City apartment on a Saturday morning. There is a bandage around his neck and his left leg is in a cast. Thelma brings him a drink while he is reading a book. There is a knock on the door. It is Wick and Doc coming for a visit. They have brought flowers and books. Roseanne joins Thelma as the four sit down.

"Hello, Doctors," says Harry.

"Hello, Harry," says Wick as he hands Harry an envelope.

"We've brought a card from camp. All the boys have signed it and they all wish you a quick recovery."

"How are you feeling?" asks Doc.

"Not so good," replics Harry. "I can't do much walking without help. But I really miss finishing the year on the island."

"We miss you too," replies Wick. "Remember, you will heal and have your senior year in high school to look forward to."

"I'm not looking forward to being a cripple at school," admits Harry. "They say I won't be able to be off crutches for a long time, and I might never walk normally again. I wish this hadn't happened. I thought I was doing all the right things. And now this."

"Harry, you have done all the right things," assures Doc. "Life is not always fair, but things eventually work out." Doc pauses to put together the right words. "I want to tell you something that no one else knows, Harry. I think your father was the soldier who saved my life in Burma."

Harry is stunned by the revelation but shows no outward emotion.

"I think it was your dad," Doc continues, "who shot a Japanese soldier who was about to kill me and a soldier whose wounds I was treating. Your father was a real hero, and you should be proud."

Harry is speechless.

"I owe him a debt of gratitude that I can never repay. But I promise you, Harry, I will do everything I can to help you achieve the success you deserve. But you have to make me a promise."

"What's that?" Harry asks, his voice breaking.

"Promise me you will do your best to never forget what a great man you father was and honor his legacy in any way you can. One way you can do this is to always do the right thing and never give up."

Harry is now breaking down into uncontrollable sobs as Thelma and Roseanne come close to comfort him.

"Have patience Harry," assures Doc, "good things will come your way."

After a few moments, Harry recomposes himself as he shares the Camp Dyer card with Thelma and Roseanne. And there is a smile as the two doctors bid goodbye.

As Wick and Doc walk from the Thompson apartment, they are silent. Doc wonders to himself if he might have gone too far in his speech to Harry.

"The major hasn't yet confirmed your hunch about Harry's father, has he?" asks Wick.

Doc smiles and nods but there are no words.

On Dyer Island, work by the boys on the walls of the mess hall is nearly completed. They are built with a generous number of frames for windows which will be installed last. But the big challenge is on how to raise the twenty-six roof trusses which they have put together on the ground. The trusses are very bulky and heavy to manage without the help of a crane.

The boys artfully figure out a mechanism to get the job done. By using a heavy rope tied to one end of a truss they pull it up slowly through a pully to the top of the wall. The bottom end is fastened to the top of the wall with heavy rope. Then the other side is brought up leaving the truss upside-down. A temporary two-by-four "wall" is built at one end of the building taller than the truss being pulled up. It has a pulley system attached to the top. With both sides fastened temporarily to the top of the wall, a rope is tied to the top of the upside-down truss as four boys raise it up six feet and other boys on the other side pull the rope through the pullies until it stands and is quickly braced in position with temporary supports. The bottoms are then properly fastened. This is repeated for the other trusses. But over four days the boys only manage to install three of the twenty-six trusses.

When Doc returns after a week of work at Lahey he is disappointed at the slow progress.

"The boys are hard at work and doing the best they can," offers Bill. "Their ingenuity is great, but they simply don't have the engineering equipment."

"Okay," says Doc who realizes the difficulty the boys face. "Let's go to plan B."

Doc goes to the mainland to use his connections. A couple of days later, an engineering crew arrives with a crane built on heavy metal tracks like a bulldozer. At low tide it is maneuvered over to the construction site. The rest of the trusses are installed in five days.

Things are all going well with the work progressing at a brisk pace when something unexpected happens to Doc. He is experiencing a heavy feeling in his chest as another day of work is beginning. There's also a pain running from his lower right arm up to the top of his throat prompting him to consult Wick about it.

"When did you first begin feeling these pains?" asks Wick.

"Off and on for some time," says Doc. "But never this intense."

Wick is checking his heart with a stethoscope.

"I don't like the sound or rhythm," pronounces Wick. "You really need to be checked out in Ellsworth."

"I'll be okay," says Doc unconvincingly.

"I insist," says Wick.

The police boat is readied by the boat crew and, with one of the boys piloting, Doc and Wick head out to Wyman's Landing followed by a thirty-minute drive to Ellsworth General.

Forty-minutes later, Doc has been given an electrocardiogram and is examined by a cardiologist.

"Doc, you've had a heart attack," says the physician.

"How can that be?" questions Doc. "I'm only 35."

"Age doesn't offer any guarantees," says the doctor. "Your blood cholesterol is very high and you should lose a few pounds. Does your family have a history of heart issues?"

"My father died of a stroke when he was sixty-two. I suppose that's history."

"Indeed, it is. Do you smoke?"

"Used to," says Doc. "Gave that up three years ago."

"Good to hear. And the good news is that your attack doesn't appear to be severe because your heart's function and rhythm seem to be returning to normal. Meantime, I'm putting you on a blood thinner and suggest you lighten your load and change your eating habits. I want to keep you overnight for observation, just in case."

"Do what good medicine dictates," says Doc. "And thanks for your honesty."

Doc is thinking there is no way he's going to cut back on the food he loves and his lust for work.

Doc returns to the island the next afternoon and is pleased to see the boys laying planking on the roof. They're installing roofing shingles on the roof deck two days later. Pre-made windows and doors arrive from the mainland. There are many finishing touches that remain for next season, but the mess hall is now a reliable shelter that can be used on a daily basis. A rough kitchen is put together quickly using whatever is on hand to build shelving for food. Tables are set up for food preparation and an outdoor grill is used for cooking. There is still no refrigeration, but the boys make do with regular ice shipments from Milbridge.

Even though the mess hall still needs finishing touches, it's decided that a new, smaller building should also be constructed to house a separate space for the infirmary. The infirmary in the lodge is too small for beds and does not allow any separation between well and sick boys or overnight stays. The new infirmary is built on an existing foundation laid for another project that had been abandoned. With that head start, more experience under their belts, and adding Saturdays to their work schedule the boys complete the new infirmary very quickly allowing the nurse to move in right away even though finishing touches would be completed the following year. The camp Citizens Band radio is also moved to the infirmary which becomes a central location for communications.

Louise, the nurse, becomes a great asset as the boys come to her for any of their ongoing medications or to be treated for any minor scrapes or cuts they might have gotten. She also is a sort of freelance therapist, offering them moral support when they need it.

"I feel like a mother confessor at times," she says, "They just want someone to talk with, for some guidance and advice."

After a couple weeks, Louise gets to know the boys, as well as their peccadillos. Knowing all of them by first names is pretty easy. But this year there are five Jimmys at camp. It's important not to mix the Jimmys up because several of them have medications she holds for various reasons. So, every Jimmy is also referred to with a last initial. Jimmy Flynn becomes Jimmy F. There is also Jimmy D, Jimmy S, Jimmy U, and Jimmy V.

Fifteen-year-old Jimmy F comes in with a scrape on his lower leg that has caused a red rash. It's trying to bleed but can't. It's just oozing. And it also hurts.

"Hello Jimmy F," says Louise. "What can I do for you today?"

"Hi Louise, I hurt my leg. They sent me to you."

If it were up to Doc, he would send Jimmy down to the water to soak his leg for fifteen minutes in the saltwater. But Louise realizes Jimmy needs something more. He is also clearly homesick.

Louise puts an antiseptic cream over the wound and a light bandage over it to keep it clean.

"Can I stay for a little while?" Jimmy asks.

"Sit there and see if you can figure out this puzzle," says Louise.

She's big on puzzles, mostly crosswords, and never misses *The New York Times* Sunday crossword. The paper is brought over to her by the boat crew from the in-town house every Sunday afternoon. In this case, Louise hands Jimmy a book of crosswords and turns to a blank one that hasn't been filled out. Jimmy takes his time and enjoys one of the candies that Louise keeps on hand. He leaves about forty-minutes later with the puzzle half done. Louise puts his name on the page. "You can finish it the next time you come by."

"Thanks, Louise."

Mission accomplished for Jimmy F.

Frank, who is sixteen, is having a hard time with his bunk mate. "Can't sleep at night," he says.

"What appears to be the problem?" she asks.

"Snoring," says Frank. "Sam usually gets to sleep right away, and when he does, he begins to sound like a buzz saw, cutting through an endless supply of two-by-fours."

"Learn to get used to it," says Louise. "Soon it will be the background noise you expect, and it won't keep you awake. In the meantime, try these".

Louise hands Frank a pair of earplugs with a piece of candy and he goes away happy.

Johnny F, not to be mixed up with Johnny A, comes in having lost one of his contact lenses. Louise keeps some extra ones in a small cubby with his name on it.

Others come to get their daily medications that are held under lock and key by Louise.

All of the boys are also drawn to the infirmary because of Pie, a large but well-mannered Newfie, a fixture on the rug next to the rocker on which Louise often sits to knit. Pie is often seen roaming around the island with Inky, the other Newfie, and the boys love them wherever they are. Sometimes they can be seen chumming it up with the harbor seals who like to sun on the rocks at low tide. Pie has a fondness for getting into the water and sometimes swimming among the seals. That has caused a minor concern because of fears Pie could be mistaken in the water for one of the seals. There is a five-dollar bounty on seals because, for obvious reasons, they are an enemy of local fishermen.

There are no more serious accidents that summer, and the doctors and camp directors are determined to keep it that way.

Wick, Anne, and Doc stagger their time between work as physicians and island life. Often, when Doc is on the island Wick and Anne are not, and vise versa. But there are always other adult supervisors who can be called on for help and emergencies. When they return from being away, they marvel at the progress made by the boys between visits. As summer is ending, it is time for banquet weekend once again with families and friends visiting their sons on the island.

Jerry Wysinger is pushing Harry in his wheelchair, alongside Thelma and Roseanne.

"We missed you," says Jerry, "and we hope you can come back next summer."

"I don't think so," replies Harry. "The doctors say I won't be able to do any heavy work and walking will still be a struggle."

"Don't let 'em tell you what you can do," counters Jerry.

"Yeah, but the doctors have been right so far," says Harry. "When I overdo it, it sets back my recovery."

"Even if you don't go back to camp you're hoping to go to college, right?" asks Jerry.

"Nah," says Harry. "We don't have the money for that."

"We'll see," says Thelma who still struggles but doesn't want to let Harry down. "We'll do the best we can."

The newly built and slightly unfinished mess hall is crowded with people as a lobster dinner is being served. There is a long head table with Wick, Doc, and other staff and special guests. Harry, with his crutches, is also seated there along with Thelma and Roseanne.

After dinner is finished, it is time to talk about accomplishments and recognize outstanding efforts. As they had the year before, it gives the boys a chance to brag about their summer accomplishments. Southy is recognized as "hardest worker" and Jerry is elected boy director for the coming year. Doc stands up to speak.

"I hope you all join me in feeling proud about a successful summer at Camp Dyer. I know you all have also been missing Harry like we have. Travel is not easy for him, but we are pleased to have Harry with us today."

The boys cheer with a standing ovation for Harry as he is helped to his feet with his crutches and waves.

"I am also thrilled to make a special announcement," Doc continues. "We've gotten word from the Bank of New York that it will underwrite our first annual college scholarship to a camper who has become an outstanding leader. Our board of directors has decided to award that first scholarship to Harry Thompson."

Everyone gets up and cheers Harry once again.

"Harry," continues Doc, "you were the very first camper and first boy director, and we can't think of anyone more deserving. This scholarship is special because it means you will be able to attend the

New York State public college of your choice and all expenses will be paid."

Thelma and Roseanne are both surprised and thrilled by the announcement as they hug Harry once again. Thelma has tears in her eyes as the boys continue to cheer and Harry blushes from ear to ear.

Harry, Thelma, and Roseanne are the last to leave the island following the banquet. Jerry accompanies them as they are ferried back to Wyman's Landing at dark. On the way back, Jerry and the boy piloting the boat use a search light aboard the boat to help their navigation. As they are about to enter the cove to the Dyer Island Pier, they spot strangers in a small boat looking over the side as if they are searching for something. Jerry calls out. "Are you looking for something? Can we help? We're from Camp Dyer and that's our dock over there."

The strangers say nothing but continue to stare down into the water. As Jerry looks down into the water he sees an amazing sight. There are hundreds of tiny flashing lights moving around in the water. The lights appear to be caused by friction created by the motion of hundreds, maybe thousands of fish. After Jerry and the boy pilot continue to be ignored by the strangers, they head for the pier and dock the police boat for the night. Jerry sees Wick when he goes into the lodge.

"There are some men out by the mouth of our cove. We saw them when we came back from taking Harry and his family. They were looking into the water and we saw these lights, like coming from thousands of fish, but the men wouldn't answer our questions about what they were up to."

"Bioluminescence," says Wick. "It comes out when an algae bloom of plankton is disturbed by fish. I've seen it in our bay. As for the men, I don't know what that could be about, but we'll look out for them in the morning."

Chapter Fourteen
Issues and Resolutions

The next morning after the incident with the strangers at the mouth of the cove, there are several small and larger boats at anchor across the entire cove surrounding the Camp Dyer pier. Wick walks down to the water from the lodge and approaches a crewman aboard one of the larger boats.

"Hello," shouts Wick. "We run this boys' camp on this island and are curious about what your intentions are at the mouth of our cove."

"None of your business," the man shouts back. "We're seine fishermen and plan to net your cove at high tide tomorrow. We'll be out of your way when we haul in our catch."

"That's a problem for us," shouts back Wick. "Our camp is closing for the summer tomorrow, and we'll need this cove open to run our shuttle back and forth."

"None of our concern," he shouts back. "We've got a schedule to keep as we move up the coast."

"I'm a camp director," shouts Wick. "Can we work out some arrangement?"

The man on the boat does not respond and goes about his work organizing the nets. As Wick walks back up toward the lodge another man appears on the bow of another fisherman's boat and holds a rifle. He fires a shot that misses Wick but crashes through a window at the lodge. Wick rushes back to the lodge to see if everyone is okay.

"Anybody hurt in there?" Wick calls.

"A window shattered," says a boy inside. "But nobody was in that room."

Wick is furious. He goes into the lodge and grabs the flare gun, goes back outside, and fires it into the air like a warning shot. The flare sounds like a cannon explosion. Wick fires another, thinking it might also summon help from the mainland.

Within a few minutes after Wick fires the flares, Glenn Flynn's boat joined by three others arrives at the mouth of the cove. They stage sort of a standoff between the seiners and the pier. Several more local fishmen then arrive and stand their ground, protecting the entrance to the cove. About a half hour goes by and suddenly, to the delight of Wick and the boys watching on the shore, the engines of the seiners' boats start up, they pull anchors, and head out for other waters. There are cheers from the boys on the shore, and Glenn waves and sounds his horn as other local boats join in. The boats stay at the mouth of the cove a while longer to make sure the seiners don't return.

The confrontation between Harry and Jerry that first summer at camp has turned into a lasting friendship. In the early fall, Harry is paying a visit to Jerry at his home in Riverdale, New York, off the northern tip of Manhattan. Even though Harry still needs a cane to assist his walking, Jerry is certain he will be fine learning now to ride one of his bikes. Harry takes the IRT subway from Hells Kitchen to 242nd Street station near Van Cortlandt Park in the Bronx just two blocks from the Wysinger House. It's a neighborhood of large Tudor-style houses and manicured green lawns seemingly a world away from Harry's neighborhood. Harry comes to the front door and rings the bell. A woman, dressed like a maid, answers the door.

"You must be Harry," she says.

"Yes, ma'am."

"Jerry's expecting you. Have a seat, he'll be right down."

In the neighboring room, the judge sits on a sofa reading a newspaper and pays no attention to Harry.

"Harry," calls Jerry as he scampers down the staircase steps. "You ready to ride?"

"Don't know," replies Harry, "but I'll give it a try."

"It's a cinch," says Jerry. "Let's go to the garage and I'll show you what we've got."

The two go out back to a large double door garage that houses the family car on one side and all manner and sizes of bikes, trikes and buggies. Among the playthings are two Schwinn bicycles.

"I'll take this one, and you take the other," says Jerry.

Harry takes hold of the bike and realizes he can use it instead of the cane to keep him steady.

"Not sure how to get started," says Harry who is hesitant.

"No sweat," replies Jerry. "Let's walk the bikes over to Van Cortlandt Park where there's no traffic and lots of wide-open space."

The two cross a pedestrian bridge that goes directly into the park.

"You can learn to ride just like I did when my dad taught me," says Jerry. "The secret is to ease your fear of falling and put centrifugal force to work. So, let's start on this gentle slope of grass where it won't hurt even if you fall over. The secret," adds Jerry, "is to steer gently in the direction you are falling. You don't have to peddle at all. Once you balance your steering the force will be with you. I won't ride. I'll just follow you along on foot."

Harry straddles the bike frame and Jerry gives him a gentle push forward. Harry takes a hard right into the ground but sticks his foot out to break the fall. He does it again and falls on the left side. Then he achieves a shaky balance before going down again.

"I think I can feel it!" Harry exclaims. "I just need a little practice."

After a few more tries, Harry is now gently steering right and left and gliding on two wheels.

"I've got it!" Harry says excitedly.

"You've got it!" shouts Jerry.

Harry works on his peddling and learns to use the brake by peddling backward. Soon, Jerry is biking alongside Harry and they head to a lightly trafficked path in the park. Nearly an hour later the two are now walking their bikes back across the pedestrian bridge over to Jerry's house. Harry is all smiles with his newfound skill.

"Why don't you come back next week when we can take a longer ride?" asks Jerry.

"Sure," says Harry who now follows Jerry back into the garage to park the bikes.

"Join me for a soda and a snack?" asks Jerry.

Harry picks up his cane where he left it and the two go in and into a room that looks like the judge's study.

"Sit down," says Jerry, "I'll be back in a minute."

Nearly ten minutes pass and all of a sudden, Judge Thomas Wysinger enters. Harry is frozen and fearful about what the judge might say to him.

"Mr. Thompson," says the judge, "you've turned quite the page. And I owe you a debt of gratitude."

"Why is that?" asks Harry.

"Jerry tells me about all the things you've done at Camp Dyer and the things you taught him. He's now proud of his own accomplishments, thanks to you. I have to admit that I misjudged you from the start. I somehow missed seeing the fine young man you really are."

Harry is relieved and doesn't quite know what to say.

"Thank you, sir."

"Just call me Thomas, as long as we're not in court," he says with a chuckle. "I don't expect I'll ever see you there again."

"Yes sir," says Harry. "Heading for college in the fall. State University of New York in Brooklyn."

"Jerry tells me you have received a scholarship," says the judge. "Congratulations, son."

Jerry returns and invites Harry into the kitchen where the table is filled with more than a snack but a full lunch of soup, salad, sandwiches, and a pineapple upside-down cake.

Jerry returns to Camp Dyer the next summer and continues for three more, becoming a senior counselor. Harry decides against coming back because of his continued need of a cane. He doesn't want to be limited in his physical activities. He spends his time, instead, reading and concentrating on his college studies. Nearly four years after Harry's chainsaw accident, he is about to graduate from State University of New York in Brooklyn.

It's a Saturday morning and Anne and Wick are home in their New York apartment. Anne brings in the daily mail, which includes a graduation invitation.

"How nice!" Anne exclaims. "Harry is graduating from SUNY Brooklyn."

"Bachelor of science, with honors!" says Wick as he reads it. "The ceremony is three weeks from today and we simply can't miss it."

Doc, at his house in Stockton, opens a similar invitation. "I'll be damned," he says out loud to himself. "He did it."

Doc remembers his promise to Harry to do anything he can to ensure his success.

I wonder if he is considering medical school? Doc thinks.

Doc, Wick, and Anne are among those arriving for Harry's commencement ceremonies. They meet Thelma and Roseanne before going inside to be seated.

"Great to see you all," says Thelma.

"Wouldn't miss it," says Wick. "And how are you doing Roseanne?"

"Great," she says smiling broadly. "I'm now a sophomore at lower SUNY, thanks to Doc's help."

"Wasn't much," says Doc. "Roseanne just needed a letter of recommendation for a scholarship. She's a great student."

They all are seated together in a huge auditorium that is nearly filled. As the graduates file in, Thelma stands up and cheers beaming with pride when Harry enters. As she takes a few pictures with a Brownie camera she catches Harry's eye, he waves, and Roseanne stands and waves back with Thelma. Harry is in a class of more than eight hundred graduates where there are few faces of color. Harry has had to overcome obstacles along the way and decided long ago to work doubly hard to make sure he deserved whatever accomplishments he achieved without question. There is no such thing as affirmative action.

His success is the result of hard work, raw talent, and looking the other way when confronted with an occasional act of discrimination.

Following the ceremonies, all seven are seated at a nearby restaurant for a celebratory meal.

"You've graduated with honors, Harry," says Doc. "How does it feel?"

"Good," says Harry, "but I'm not tired of school yet."

"It's a great accomplishment," offers Anne. "Many of your courses were pre-med. Does that mean what we think it means?"

"The difficult we do at once," replies Harry with a chuckle.

"The impossible takes a little longer," echoes Doc. "Where have I heard that before? If your sights are on medical school, we think we can help. Between me, Wick, and Anne, you have a lot of connections."

"If you think I'm good enough, I'd like to explore that possibility."

"Just imagine," says Thelma, "my son, the doctor."

"Not beyond reach for you," adds Doc. "I'll be happy to do whatever I can."

A couple of days later, Doc calls Harry from his home in Brockton, Massachusetts.

"Hello Harry, how does Columbia University School of Medicine sound to you?"

"Is that possible for me?" replies Harry. "Isn't that school difficult to get into?"

"Yes," says Doc, "but you have a lot to offer them, and they'll recognize that. You qualify for special consideration as a minority, and between Wick and me you would be mentored. I spoke with one of my connections at Columbia and he thinks you would meet their requirements."

"They're in the Bronx, not far from where we live," says Harry. "I could easily commute to cut costs."

"That's right," says Doc. "I've asked them to send you forms and all the information you should need. And I'll help you fill it out if needed. You should get them in a few days and let me know when you do."

"You bet I will," says Harry. "Thank you so much!"

After Harry hangs up, his thoughts run wild. He thinks of the time he was trying to sell contraband cigarettes, when he accosted

Wick in desperation, was given a chance by the doctors to go to the island, about learning that he could accomplish great things with his hands and some ingenuity, that scary things like standing up to Jerry could bring about positive results. He also recalls those awful days at Lavenburg when at his lowest point he decided to bury himself in books and open up a new world of understanding. Then, he thinks about his father, Thelma, and Roseanne and how proud he would be to make them proud.

Harry is weeks into the exciting yet daunting task of applying for the four-year program for medical doctors at Columbia. He knows that thousands apply yet only about four percent get accepted. With Doc's tutelage, Harry is completing five essays that deal with his goals, work history while attending college, how he has displayed and used leadership, how his minority background can be harnessed to the betterment of all, and how he can channel his profession as a medical doctor to benefit his immediate community. He undergoes a faculty interview and a student interview. He receives recommendation letters from Doc, Wick, Anne, and a couple of Columbia physicians Doc knows.

He must also be vetted as a good, law-abiding citizen and certify that he has no criminal past. This last point is a concern to Harry because of his involvement with New York police and juvenile court even though he has been assured that this record has been expunged from the system. Harry completes the process and now it's a waiting game for a response from Columbia admissions.

Several weeks pass and finally a letter arrives from Columbia. It's not a packet as one might expect if accepted. It's a one-page letter which Harry is afraid to open. But he must of course. The diplomatic formality of the words in the letter are of no point because of the few that really matter.

"Your application for enrollment in the fall semester is declined because of a juvenile criminal file provided by New York Juvenile Court."

Harry's heart sinks and all his visions of grandeur awash. He composes himself for a telephone call to Doc in Brockton.

"This must be a mistake," Doc assures. "We will figure out a way to clear this up. You know Jerry whose father was the judge involved in your case. Before I get involved, call your friend Jerry to find out what his father says about it."

"Okay," says Harry, "I'll try."

Harry calls the Wysinger home hoping to reach Jerry.

"Hello, Wysinger residence," says a woman's voice answering the telephone.

"Is Jerry home?" asks Harry.

"I'm afraid not. Who am I speaking with?" she asks.

"I'm Harry Thompson, Jerry's friend from Camp Dyer. I'm afraid I have a problem and was hoping that Jerry could speak with his father about it."

"Well, Jerry won't be home for a couple of weeks, but let me see if I can get the judge to speak with you."

Harry is gripped in fear as he waits.

"Harry, this is Thomas Wysinger. Doreen says you have a problem. Is it something I can help you with?"

"I hope so, sir," says Harry. "I have applied for Columbia Medical School."

"That's wonderful, son!"

"But they have a problem with a record that exists on me from the court. I thought all of that went away."

"Oh, I'm sorry to hear that. I don't know how they were given a record that was to be filed away."

There is a moment of silence and Harry feels like his heart is pounding loud enough to be heard over the telephone.

"I'll tell you what I'm going to do," says Judge Wysinger. "I will go to the clerk in the morning and see what we can do about this. If necessary, I'll write a letter on your behalf."

"That would be greatly appreciated," says Harry.

Harry calls Doc back and tells him what the judge has promised.

"That should do the trick," Harry. But college admissions is a bureaucratic nightmare. I'll also reach out to my contacts at Columbia to explain what happened."

Harry's disappointment is now replaced by hope.

But hope never gets anyone anywhere, Harry thinks. *I must follow up in any way I can to get my shot at med school.*

Doc follows through with his connections and a letter is sent by Judge Wysinger to Columbia admissions. The ball is now in the court of Columbia University admissions.

Chapter Fifteen
The Years

Older Harry continues his walk along Dyer Island trails with Wick and Johnny while telling the story of Camp Dyer.

"Jerry would continue his involvement at Camp Dyer over the next several years. Events at the camp would be repeated year after year as the population gradually grew to 60 and served generations of boys just like you Johnny. Boys became plumbers when pipes connected the buildings they constructed. After gas generators were brought in, boys were appointed to a power crew and some of them learned to be electricians and wired island buildings to bring island life into more modern times."

"Boys like me wired the island with electricity?" asks Johnny as his interest seems to be piqued.

"That's right," says Harry.

The Camp Dyer Foundation purchases a brand-new twenty-foot Boston Whaler to supplement the old police boat for travel back and forth from the mainland. In 1960, Anne and Wick bring their first child, Walter Junior, into the world, followed three years later by Mary Anne. Walter Junior and Mary Anne become intensely involved in Camp Dyer as they get older. Mary Anne helps take care of the business and organize fundraising during the off season while Walt, who began as a camper at fourteen, becomes a camp counselor, later senior counselor working with the boy directors every year, and finally adult advisor.

Wick and Doc, with the help of Walt and Mary Anne, begin to work on ways to raise money off season for the camp's operation. They vow to continue free tuition to boys from families that can't afford to pay expenses.

Doc sets up a camp headquarters at his Brockton, Massachusetts home and holds meetings with boys in the fall and winter months to plan camp activities for the coming year. There is also a focus on fundraising activities including running a haunted house on Halloween, selling wreaths and Christmas trees in December, and other such efforts.

The Wyman Company which runs Wyman's Landing and a sardine factory is also involved in cultivating and marketing Maine blueberries. Doc thinks it would be a great idea for Camp Dyer to purchase some land on the mainland for future blueberry harvests. There, undeveloped and abandoned land could be had at a very low cost and so Doc purchases several acres on behalf of Camp Dyer. For several years during weekend trips and throughout the summer, Camp Dyer boys work to clear out the old growth like red pines that had since taken over abandoned fields to create new locations for the planting of blueberries. The clearing work is slow and difficult but the boys work at it diligently. While low-bush blueberries grow wild on the island and the mainland, producing a regular crop with commercial viability is another matter. Weather and irrigation are problems to be overcome. Since there are freshwater ponds in the area, there must be viable groundwater, which can be tapped by a well. Unfortunately attempts at digging wells down to as much as ninety feet are unsuccessful.

As the old saw goes, "if you can't beat 'em, join 'em." Doc realizes boys can also make real money for the camp and spending money for themselves by picking berries in Wyman's fields. And so, for a couple of weeks out of the eight-week camp season, groups of boys camp out nearby and work the fields. The labor is hot and backbreaking. The boys use blueberry rakes, which look like oversized dustpans with long tines, to grab the berries off the bushes planted in four-foot-wide rows. Once a boy fills his rake, he dumps the berries into five-gallon buckets. Once full, the buckets are carried to a machine that separates leaves from berries and washes them before they are loaded into blueberry trays. Each tray yields three dollars for the camp and twenty-five cents to the boy harvester. In a good day a boy could earn nearly ten dollars with nearly a hundred dollars going to Camp Dyer.

Starting a Christmas tree farm is another idea put into action by Doc. Up until this time, trees were purchased from farms in Canada and re-sold at a profit at a stand in Massachusetts. The program is a success, but Doc knows if the Camp grows its own trees they will make even more profit from it. He meets with several of the camp boys and a couple of adult supervisors at the end of the summer season. They have volunteered to stay on for an extra ten days to close-up the camp for the winter and plant the trees.

Binocs is the youngest among the eight boys and two adult supervisors staying on.

"I've managed to purchase ten thousand balsam fir seedlings," says Doc to the group. "When fully grown in seven to eight years, they will become Christmas trees free of additional expense to sell at our Christmas fundraisers."

"Where will we plant them?" asks Fred, a former camper and now adult supervisor.

"We're driving to Cherryfield Road," says Doc, "where there are grassy fields that the owner has agreed to allow us to use as a tree farm."

Doc shows the boys and the men exactly what they need to do to successfully plant each tree.

"You take a spade, push hard enough on it with your foot to cut through the thick grass. You force the spade forward enough to open a space several inches wide, insert just the four-inch-long roots, allowing the rest of the foot-tall seedling to stand free and straight, pull out the blade and tamp the ground a bit. It's that easy. Then you just take two medium steps forward, about four feet, and repeat along lines laid out in the field."

With ten people doing the work, each person would need to repeat this operation a thousand times.

"That sounds like something we can realistically accomplish," says Fred. "It'll just take several days."

The men and boys set up camp near the fields. Doc has managed to gather enough supplies for a week. So, the work begins.

By the third day, the volunteer field workers are getting tired and still have more than six thousand seedlings to put in the ground. They soldier on. But Binocs, working on the far end of the other side of the field, has an idea to speed up the process.

What if I plant two trees in each hole? he thinks. *All of them likely won't survive anyway. If I plant two at least one is practically guaranteed to survive.*

By the end of the fifth day, and dog-tired, the ten men and boys finally finish their labor. But Doc, looking over the field of work, discovers Binocs' questionable method. Doc approaches Binocs closely and looks straight into his eyes.

"Binocs," Doc says firmly. "Did I show you precisely how each tree should be planted?"

"Yes sir."

"Did you follow my directions like the others did?"

"No sir."

"When I bought these seedlings, did I expect that half of them would never survive?"

"No sir."

"Did you let me and the others down in executing your part of the project?"

"Yes sir."

"Can you explain your actions?"

"I was getting tired. And I thought I could speed things up."

"If we," Doc replies, "are called upon to do our part for the Camp Dyer community, do we do it halfway?"

"No sir. I'm sorry. I understand now."

"That's all I ask," says Doc. "And that's all we expect. If you or anyone else is having difficulty, what do we do?"

"Ask for help," replies Binocs.

"That's all we expect, son. I'm confident that next time you will," replies Doc as he pats Binocs on the shoulder and shakes his hand.

Doc drops the subject and moves on to other things. Binocs, without being asked, heads back to the field to right his wrongs. When the others find out, they decide to join in to help him finish the job. Binocs now has newfound respect for his peers and the knowledge that when Doc asks him to do something, he means to do it with one hundred percent effort. Binocs also learns that a job well done earns the respect from members of the Camp Dyer community.

Doc is always direct and honest with the boys, no matter how young. He always begins conversations with "How's it going?" and expects a truthful and honest reply showing genuine interest in their response. "What do you think of the camp? How can we improve it? What are your concerns? Do you have another idea on how to get this done?" These words come with direct eye contact and an expectation that the conversation will be brought to a satisfying conclusion. He gives each boy a sense that he is important, and Doc's respect is returned in loyalty.

Another fundraising effort by the boys is creating and staging a haunted house during the days and nights around Halloween. The boys truly love to do it, from the art of designing costumes and performing realistic monster skits.

While Doc concentrates on entrepreneurial schemes to raise funds, Wick concentrates on tapping the resources available in New York City society. He spends his time in the off months contacting potential donors through social and hospital circles. Running a summer camp for challenged teen boys has great appeal for potential donors.

Many of Wick's patients at Roosevelt Hospital are quite wealthy and influential. Wick never misses an opportunity to talk about his work with the boys at Camp Dyer and word gets around. One of Wick's wealthy connections is Maria Moore, an elderly widow who had become an annual contributor to the Camp Dyer Foundation. On one occasion, Wick brought Walt Jr. and one of the Camp Dyer boys with him to pay a visit to Mrs. Moore at her Park Avenue apartment.

"Wick, it's so nice to see you. And hello, Walt. And who is this other nice-looking young man you've brought with you?" she asks.

"This is Frederick Simpson, but I believe you met him at camp last year."

"Oh Freddy," she says. "Of course, now I remember."

Mrs. Moore gives Wick a hug and then Walt. Fred holds out his hand expecting a handshake, but she gives him a big hug instead.

"It's so nice to see you all," she says, "you must tell me about some of the new things you boys have planned for this summer. Come in and make yourselves comfortable while I prepare some tea."

In ten minutes, Maria arrives back in the sitting room with a tray of tea and cookies.

"No new buildings planned so far" says Walt. "We will be re-roofing the lodge and some of the cabins."

"I'm a mentor to the younger boys," says Fred. "We try to teach new skills, like electrical wiring and plumbing. In addition to work projects, the boys will be learning sailing and motorboat management."

"Will we see you again this summer?" asks Walt.

"God willing, I'll be back in Milbridge," she replies.

Mrs. Moore has made a habit of visiting Milbridge House Hotel during the past several summers, and Wick always makes sure she is given a tour of island projects. She also owns a good deal of land in Maine. The most prominent parcel is Cape Split, fifteen miles north of Milbridge, comprised of several-hundred-acres surrounded by ocean on all four sides except for a narrow causeway that connects to the mainland. It is lightly developed and considered prime real estate.

On Sundays, Walt and Doc make sure a couple of the Protestant camp boys escort Mrs. Moore from the hotel across the street to attend services at the First Congregational Church while some other boys go to First Methodist for their interdenominational services. After the service, Mrs. Moore invites all of the boys to lunch at the Red Barn.

A year after Wick, Walt, and Fred's visit, Mrs. Moore dies. And in her will, she bequeaths Cape Split to the Camp Dyer Boys Foundation. The sale of Cape Split allows the Foundation to purchase a house in Milbridge at Wayman's Landing that becomes "the in-town house," where the camp has a small dock, houses laundry facilities, a CB radio, and a telephone to enhance camp communications. It also allows for the purchase of a Camp Dyer headquarters for off-season work in West Bridgewater, Massachusetts, and even a school bus to provide camp transportation for mainland outings.

As the camp infrastructure evolves, much of the work by the boys becomes necessary maintenance such as installing new roofs on aging structures and there is always the need for repairing and replacing weathered planking on the main pier. New boys are encouraged to plan and build new cabins. Each plan is considered by the elders and when approved the boys are allowed to work on their projects on nights and weekends. Finishing a cabin might take several years and some boys have no patience for that, so Doc came up with an ingenious solution. Any boy or boys who complete a cabin will have the privilege of its use for the rest of their lives. And the fact that it takes several years to complete a cabin brings boys back to camp year after year. As the boys' skills grow so grows the camp infrastructure.

Then there are new projects which would have been considered unnecessary in the early days. One such project is to build a forty-by-eighty foot saltwater swimming pool because the water while swimming off the cove is always at an intolerable temperature of fifty five degrees. With the building of a pool and the use of an endless supply of seawater, the sun itself would take care of the temperature issue making swimming more of a sport and leisure activity so the boys can sooth their tired muscles.

Digging the hole for the pool is a big challenge. Doc acquires a fifty-year-old diesel bulldozer that had been in the hold of a ship that transports tar and is no longer needed. The earth-moving monster works very well a great deal of the time but with one major glitch. One of the wheels that drives the right track is a bit out of line, so it regularly throws off the heavy iron track it was designed to drive. Each time the track is dislodged requires an hour or more labor to get it back in place. Just another challenge for the camp motto, "The difficult we do at once, the impossible takes a little longer."

When the hole is finally dug, the next challenge is building the pool walls out of cement blocks. Finally, the pouring of the concrete floor requires the most intense and continuous labor. The floor is poured directly onto the granite foundation which had been cleaned with seawater. The entire floor is a four-day effort of pouring concrete which is continuously being mixed by hand. A new section of concrete is poured before the last section dries ensuring a good bond. After the entire floor is cured and dried several coats of waterproof paint is applied. Even having done all of this, the pool still leaks so fresh seawater is pumped in at every high tide. In the end, the water is kept at a comfortable sixty-five to seventy degrees. It's a little bit of Florida in Maine.

Another project is to build a landing strip for small, fixed-wing planes, a need perceived by Doc because of his long commutation routine. Doc would be on the island nearly every weekend even though he had a full schedule that kept him at the hospital from early Mondays to late Fridays. His 325-mile drive from Brockton took at least eight hours. He would drive all night, work hard with the boys for two days, then make it back to Brockton to begin a surgery at 5 a.m. on a Monday. Doc knows that if he could fly directly in a small plane his trip could easily be done in three hours and that such a landing strip would allow more easy access for visitors.

So, Doc and the boys begin the process of removing debris from a large clearing along an old logging road on the north side beyond the lodge. It's a wide-open clearing nearly three hundred yards long. Doc meets with Walt at the site to discuss the feasibility.

"The main obstacles I see," says Doc, "are the rocks and the holes."

"The rocks can be moved," says Walt. "If they're too big we can use the bulldozer. But the holes might be a problem."

"Why is that?" asks Doc.

Walt is studying engineering in college and knows a thing or two about foundations.

"The problem here is that much of the soil is very sandy," says Walt. "The holes we fill in will likely come back after the ground settles for a month or two. We don't have big trucks to bring in tons and tons of heavy landfill."

"Good point," says Doc. "Let's try to work on a section and see how we do."

A group of boys begin to work on a parcel thirty yards wide and fifty yards long. The stones don't pose a much of a problem and are easily moved over to the edges, but the holes are another matter. It seems felled trees were dumped and sunk below the old logging road years ago to prevent vehicles from sinking too much into the soil while pulling heavy loads of logs. There are hidden crevices every yard or so. The boys bring in what landfill they can find from beach stones to sand and soil and the going is very slow. But the plan comes to a screeching halt when word arrives that a similar landing strip built in nearby Cherryfield had a plane tip over when it hit a hole while landing. Hearing about the accident causes Doc to immediately drop the plan. The project then changes to building a sports field which offers a new place for touch football and other sports for the boys.

The Camp Dyer bus is heading out early on a Saturday morning for the coastal town of Bar Harbor which will include a visit to Acadia National Park. Supervising the boys are Southy, now an adult who became a successful accountant and volunteers his summers at the camp; Fred, a senior counselor; and Walt, a junior counselor. The first stop will be Punk Lake, a favorite fresh-water swimming hole for the boys. Each has brought a bar of soap and a towel so they can be fresh and clean for the visit to the upscale tourist town, a gateway to Acadia. A direct trip to Bar Harbor is nearly an hour but with time spent at the lake, they arrive at 10 a.m. With some spending money from the outside camp work, they head first to a familiar pizza place on Main Street where the boys scarf down a few slices. There are stops at some local souvenir and clothing shops.

"I'm gonna buy some new socks," declares David, rummaging through the wares at Island Outfitters.

"How about this sweatshirt?" jokes Jimmy as he reads the words Bah-Hahbah printed on the front as if to make fun of the accents of many people who visit.

"I'd rather have a moose shirt," declares David.

After roaming around for nearly an hour collecting odds and ends and loose candy, they end up at Mount Desert Ice Cream before making the short trip to the Acadia parking lot. The boys skip the welcome center as they have all been given park passes provided by Camp Dyer.

They split up to explore on their own, agreeing to meet back at the bus at 3pm. Fred, Walt, and four other boys head for the Precipice trailhead near Sand Beach where they hope to climb up sheer ledges of rocks with the help of iron rungs and be treated to one of the most astounding views of the Atlantic Ocean one thousand feet below. Precipice is closed parts of the year because Peregrine Falcons nest there. Today they're lucky because it's open. But to get onto Precipice, one has to negotiate "the eliminator." It's a boulder outcropping with two awkwardly placed iron rungs. This is a test of sorts. For anyone who has trouble or fear climbing up this obstacle, it's time to turn around. This is nothing for Dyer Island boys as Fred, Walt and the boys make it up with a couple of grunts and groans. The middle of the trail is the most dangerous.

"Wow, don't look down," shouts Walt.

"Or maybe you'd better look down," replies Fred.

A narrow path on the rock wall a couple of feet wide takes them to the cliff ledge where they must carefully balance while holding onto the rungs to get to a safer section of rock. And then they climb some more. These young men and boys are in great shape but truly exhausted when they reach the pinnacle. The sky is clear, and the water below is deep blue. There is a cruise ship seemingly the size of a mini toy anchored off the coast down below and the scene is a panaramic wonder. No words are spoken as they recover and soak it all in. It's another priceless moment deserving of a king for these regular kids who had too often experienced much less.

Before dark, the boys board the bus for the top of Cadillac Mountain which affords a 360- degree view of Acadia and a spectacular sunset. At 1,530 feet it's the highest point along the North Atlantic seaboard and among twenty other peaks on Mount Desert Island. From March to October Cadillac is the first place one can see the sunrise in the United States. One of the most striking features are the deep gouges in the bare granite at the top that follow a north-south direction as the result of the last retreating glacier about eighteen thousand years ago.

As the sun sets, the boys look to the west to witness the deep red sky and the long shadows across the waters and small islands down below.

"Never have I seen anything like this in New York," says Southy.

"I know," says Walt. "And it never gets old."

As the red turns to black, the men and boys are on the bus heading back to Milbridge and the dark ride across the bay to Dyer Island.

The success of those inaugural years would provide more scholarships to outstanding campers and becomes convincing evidence that the philosophy behind Camp Dyer is working. Most of the boys come away from the camp as responsible members of their communities back home and some end up in professions like law enforcement, law, and medicine. Others become successful in the trades. Of course, there are occasional exceptions when one camper or another engages in actions that violate the trust of the Camp Dyer community. Bringing alcohol to Camp Dyer is strictly forbidden and being caught with it more than once guarantees a one-way ticket home. Other violations allow more room for rehab as a violator is allowed to rebuild the trust of the camp community.

Breakfast is over in the dining hall on a Saturday as Richard Heff, an eighteen-year-old senior counselor, rings a bell in The Cage. It's a corner section of the mess hall by the front entrance covered in chicken wire nearly up to the rafters with a padlocked door. It's usually locked because it's where campers' valuables and private mail for the boys is kept.

"Time for mail call," calls Richard. "Some of you boys have care packages from home that arrived this week. The first one is for Billy O."

Billy comes forward to claim a small package.

"Here's one for Bobby H."

Bobby comes forward to claim his package along with a letter. Other names are called and each comes forward to claim their mail.

Outside the mess hall at 2 a.m., a fifteen-year-old boy dressed in dark clothing sneaks in. There is no one there and it is dark inside except for the headlamp he is wearing. The boy moves one of the tables to a corner next to The Cage. He places a chair on top of it and climbs up to the rafters next to the top of The Cage where the chicken wire ends. He is very athletic, carrying a rope and pulley configuration, as well as a pillowcase tied to his belt. He arranges the rope and pulley in order to lower himself down to where there are nearly a dozen packages waiting for Saturday delivery. He grabs a couple that are not too large and look promising putting them in the pillowcase. He then raises himself back up and eventually back onto the chair and climbs down to the table. He carefully puts the table and chair where they were and sneaks out the way he came in.

At dawn that morning, the "burglar" has the pillowcase and packages on his bed and has cleaned up. He is Donnie, a bit of a loner among the boys. In his upper bunk, he empties out one of the boxes. There are several pairs of sox, a pair of flip flops, candy bars, and a twenty-dollar bill. He puts on one of the pairs of socks and leaves the other box unopened. He jumps down off the bed and heads off to breakfast.

During breakfast, Donnie sits with other campers and draws a comment from one of them.

"Hey Donnie, new socks. A care package from home?"

"Yep," replies Donnie.

"Didn't see you come up to claim one," says another camper.

Donnie does not reply, but quickly finishes breakfast and gets up with his tray.

When Donnie arrives back at his cabin, he goes up to his bunk and discovers the opened package and the other one is gone. There is a knock on the door and in comes counselor Heff, holding the packages as hard evidence of the caper that Donnie has committed.

During another summer at camp, sixteen-year-old Dennis George is sitting in his bunk counting out some paper money. It's the product of his scrounging around at every opportunity picking up loose bills that he thinks won't be missed. He puts the money into an envelope, seals it, and writes his name on it. It goes into a larger envelope with a note attached and a letter home.

Later that week Charlie's mother, Charlene, is opening the daily mail. She opens the oversized letter from Charlie with news about camp life. Inside, is also the thick, sealed envelope with instructions.

"Do not open this envelope," Charlie writes. "It's for me to open when I get home later this month."

As caring mothers often do, Charlene opens the envelope anyway and find it is stuffed with paper money.

Later, Charlene is on the telephone.

"Hello, Dr. Wickson," she says. "Thank you for responding to my message and calling. I'm wondering if some campers got paying jobs while at camp this summer."

She pauses as she listens to Wick.

"Some of the boys spent some time picking blueberries on the mainland, but Charlie was not among them."

"Well then," replies Charlene, "I don't understand why Charlie sent an envelope to himself with two hundred dollars in it."

Charlie would be confronted later in the day.

The stories of camp capers are among the tales Harry recalls as he continues his walk on island paths with Wick and Johnny.

"Campers like Donnie and Dennis who got into trouble lost the respect of the others," says Harry. "Some were able to gain that trust back again. They would be put in special quarters with counselors and given a second chance. But others who didn't redeem themselves ended up being sent home."

Those stories are difficult for Johnny to hear. While he did return the items he took from a cabin a few days ago, he has yet to earn back the respect he lost. He is relieved he is not confronted about it and changes the subject with a question.

"What became of Doc?" Johnny asks.

"I'm glad you ask, Johnny," replies Harry. "Doc was a great inspiration and truly loved by the boys, every generation of them.

His involvement with Camp Dyer continued as he also served as Chief of Surgery at Goddard Hospital in Brockton, Massachusetts. That means he was really committed to the boys. To complete Doc's story, I have to take you back to 1979, when you were probably only two years old."

Walter Junior, who is now nineteen and a senior camp counselor, is addressing a new season of campers, counselors, and adult supervisors on the first day of camp.

"Now," says Walter, "I'd like to introduce Dr. Meredith Jones, who really needs no introduction for most of us, as we know him simply as Doc. Doc will tell us what we have instore for this summer."

There is applause as Doc, who has now gained weight and moves a bit slower, gets up to speak.

"I see some new faces here and am happy to welcome you to the Camp Dyer community. The campers who came before you accomplished some pretty remarkable things as you can see all around the island, including the construction of the building we're in now. But let me be clear, they weren't any more special than you. They learned skills, as you will, and pitched in on our projects to accomplish new goals. Relying on each other is how the Camp Dyer community works so well."

The lights are flickering, go out, and then come back on.

"Just ask the electrical crew manning our generators."

There is laughter.

"So here are the projects, your projects, for this summer," Doc continues. "First of all, we will be re-roofing some of the older buildings, including the lodge. That's the oldest building on the island. We'll also be asking for two volunteers to finish the fireplace at Wick and Anne's cabin."

None of the boys ever complained about working on such things without being paid because they received free training in a professional skill and were not required to pay tuition to attend Camp Dyer. The skills they learned many would use in their lives at home. It was also a therapy most of them needed to become better citizens.

"But the big project," Doc continues, "will involve constructing a new building which might prove to be the most difficult job we've ever undertaken."

Chatter can be heard among the boys.

"Are you ready for a very significant challenge?" Doc asks.

There is applause and a few boys shout things like "Yeah" and "Bring it on."

"As most of you know, last year we completed the footings for a chapel building, but we hadn't started work above the foundation. I envision this as a very special building and I want it to stand out. But, until now, we hadn't figured out the materials."

A young camper raises his hand and speaks, "Why do we need a chapel?"

Right now," continues Doc, "we have every type of building we need on this island. But we don't have a place to go when we want quiet time, a time to reflect and, yes, pray. We need a chapel. And it won't be one for any specific religion. We have Christians, Jews, Muslims and even non-believers who attend Camp Dyer. The spot which we laid out just down the hill from here has just the right exposure and an inspiring view. But I don't want this to be an ordinary building. Like great buildings such as memorials in our nation's Capital, it can't be made of just wood. A steel company has just donated a metal framework for the construction and we will build the rest with pink granite, bricks, and glass."

The boys are buzzing with discussion.

One boy shouts, "The difficult we do at once!"

There is laughter and another boy raises his hand.

"There's no such stone here," he says. "Where will we get it?"

"We can make the bricks," Doc replies, "but granite is another matter. We will be using pink granite from a quarry on Hurricane Island, 20 miles to the south. The stone has already been roughly cut and we have been given permission to take as much as we need for the building."

Another boy raises his hand.

"How will we do that?" he asks.

"That's an important question," Doc replies. "We will make trips there on Tuesdays using one of our boats towing a scow. Here's where it's going to be up to your collective ability to come up with a plan to accomplish this."

The buzzing discussion among the boys is getting louder.

"So, listen to me," Doc continues. "Will it be difficult? Yes. Is it impossible? No! This is expensive stone, and I don't think the people who run the quarry realize our true capabilities."

On a Tuesday morning before daylight, eight boys walk together to the mess hall. As they enter, there are ten bag lunches packed and placed in a box on the table along with jugs of water. Doc and Wick are already seated with Walter Junior discussing the day's plans.

As the boys sit down, Doc greets them. "Good morning, boys. It's going to be a hard day's work. Is everybody up to it?"

The boys nod yes and there are a few "yes sirs."

"We have thirty minutes before we have to leave," adds Doc. "Walt and I are going to check the line on the scow. We'll see you boys on the pier."

Doc leaves with Walt. Wick is staying behind as the boys dig in for a breakfast of scrambled eggs, gobs of bacon, and toasted bagels. There are also pitchers of Kool-Aid which has been the boys' drink of choice.

Twenty-five minutes later, Doc, Walt, and the boys head out of the cove aboard the old police boat pulling the scow twenty feet behind with a heavy line.

One of the boys is piloting the boat as it moves into open water. Two hours later, it's a bright morning in calm conditions as Doc peers through binoculars. He mutters to himself and then hands the glasses over to Walt for a view.

"Take a look," says Doc. "That's the island."

As Doc points, he moves up beside the boy piloting.

"Keep the heading at one hundred eighty degrees and we'll veer to the port side as we approach," says Doc.

As their boat and the scow arrive at Hurricane Island, it is approaching low tide as they had planned.

The planning is not simple. The tides refuse to follow a clock. Rather than being regular, the tides follow the pull of the moon. As a result, it is six and a half hours from low to high tide, and thirteen hours from high to high. This means that the time of high and low tide moves ahead by about an hour each day.

Walt grabs a long stick to check the water's depth as Doc takes over control of the boat.

"That's about as far as we can go," shouts Walt. "Okay boys, four on each side and keep her steady."

The boys' team is led by boy director Johnny Krause, the biggest and strongest among the boys, with a reputation of taking on any difficult task. They all jump out following Johnny's lead and wade in the cold water nearly up to their waists to each side of the scow as Walt unties the line from the boat. Then, the boys, led by Johnny, walk the scow over toward a tall pier as Doc and Walt pilot the boat back toward deeper water and to a small dock in a nearby cove. Doc and Walt walk over to the pier, looking down at the scow. It's now grounding in the mud as the tide continues to go lower. The boys slosh through the seaweed and mud and pull themselves up the bank by the pier with a knotted rope. They seem to know exactly what they are doing.

"Okay boys," shouts Doc. "Nice job. We're going to have to work fast."

The boys work two by two, carrying large granite stones down to the pier and dropping them into the mud below next to the scow. They are careful not to hit the scow as that could damage it. Doc and Walt work in the quarry pit with the boys. Doc tries to pick up one of the stones with one of the other boys but begs off, out of breath.

"Are you okay?" asks Johnny who is working with his teammate nearby.

"I'm alright," responds Doc. "I guess I'm pretty out of shape for this."

Walt takes Doc's place with the boy in walking the stone toward the pier. The relay continues until a significant number of granite stones have been dropped into the mud. Down below next to the scow, the boys now pick up the stones from the mud and place them carefully and evenly into the scow until all the stones are loaded. It's a very heavy load.

While waiting for the tide to rise once again, they all head back up to the pier where their lunches await.

"Good job everyone," Doc commends. "Now we just have to wait."

Nearly an hour later, the scow is beginning to float again, heavy in the water but buoyed by the rising tide. One of the boys keeping watch shouts, "She's up. She's up."

The boys head back down into the waist-deep water. With four on each side, they slowly walk the scow to deeper water while Doc and Walt power the police boat into place to re-hook the line. Johnny Krause fishes out the heavy tow line and hands it over to Doc on the boat. Doc takes the line but hesitates like something is bothering him. He then hands it over to Walt who bends over to fasten it securely to the rear of the boat. The boys pull themselves back onboard and Doc maneuvers the boat to pull the scow back out to open water. Seeing the boat slowly towing the scow is a unique sight because the weight of the granite sinks the scow so low in the water, it can't be seen on the surface. It looks as though the boat is magically towing a bunch of floating rock slabs.

Back on Dyer Island, it's getting dark as the police boat lumbers in with the scow in tow. Walt unties the scow after it is maneuvered over to the pier as close as possible. It is now nearly grounded as the boys jump out once again to push it into the muck as far as they can. Wick greets them as they tie up to the mooring.

"You're late," Wick shouts. "We were beginning to worry."

"It went well," replies Doc, "but we underestimated the time it would take getting back with that heavy load."

"We've got a late dinner waiting for you," says Wick. "We'll have a new crew unload at low tide in the morning. Good job boys!"

In the morning, the boys who went to Hurricane Island are allowed to sleep late. A new bunch of boys now carry granite stones from the grounded scow and place them on the platform of a trailer hooked up to a tractor on the shore. In a nearby grassy clearing, Johnny Krause and the boys who traveled to get the stones now engage in a game of touch football. With this hard work and plenty of time for horseplay, the Camp Dyer boys are forming a bond that few their age experience.

On another day, there will be no work at all as the Camp Dyer boys travel to the mainland to take part in a day of fun put on by the town of Milbridge. It's the annual Codfish Relay footrace held every year at the end of July as part of the small town's birthday celebration. The boys look forward to fielding a couple of teams every year. This year, it will be counselors versus boy campers as they help carry on the Milbridge tradition.

A codfish, of course, weighing in at about twenty pounds, is the star of the day and the object of the race. To make matters more difficult, the fish is covered in sardine oil and gets smellier as the relays continue. No rubber gloves are allowed and putting fingers into the gills for a better hold is forbidden. Each team is comprised of four teammates, two on each end of a thirty-yard stretch of meadow. All racers must be suited up in fireman's gear to carry the cod but there is only one set per team. It's comprised of hip boots and suspenders, a yellow slicker, and a pair of fireman's gloves. Racers have to swap into that gear to run their leg of the race, so a speedy change is also a key to winning. To make matters more entertaining, a squad of locals unleash a full-throttle jet of water on the racers from a fire hose as they pass the middle of the course with the cod. Each team is timed, and the fastest team finishing the anchor leg wins.

One important factor in codfish racing is the condition of the fish which deteriorates as the day unfolds. That's a problem when the fish is broken into more than one piece because the whole fish must finish every heat. It's a good reason to allow the youngest and less experienced racers to go in the first heats. Today, the Dyer Island Boys teams are in the middle stages along with some local merchants like the Red Barn Restaurant team. Local firemen go in the final heat.

For the Dyer Island boys, Walt Wickson leads the counselors' team and Johnny Krause leads the boy camper team. A crowd of locals line the course for their heats. The Dyer Island Counselors get off to a pretty good, yet awkward start. But Walt is stymied by tangled gear as he heads into the anchor leg. He drops the cod once in a blast of water from a firehose, but the fish is still whole as his team finishes in two minutes, twenty-nine seconds. Next are the Camp Dyer boys who manage to hold their own into the anchor leg run by Johnny. Johnny aces the change-over in record time and does not drop the cod as he is blasted with water. Their finishing time bests the counselors by two seconds. It turns out their time of two minutes, twenty-seven seconds is good enough to win this year's relays.

"How'd you change into that gear so fast? asks Walt as he and Johnny wait with the boys for the awards ceremony.

"My dad's a fireman," replies Johnny. "Where I come from firemen raise their kids to step into their shoes."

"Are you going to be a fireman?" asks Walt.

"Nah," says Johnny. "I don't know what I want to do."

As the emcee begins to announce prizes, the Red Barn Restaurant team is awarded fourth, the Milbridge Firestormers are third, and the Dyer Island boys are first and second with Johnny's team getting the top award.

"There's one more tradition we are beginning this year," announces the emcee. "The winning racer in the anchor leg gets to kiss the cod!"

Johnny is always game to go along, and puckers up to the fish with no hesitation as the crowd erupts in cheers and laughter.

Back on Dyer Island, work by the boys on the thirty-by-forty-foot chapel building gets underway even as they continue to make weekly trips to Hurricane Island for more pink granite. Under expert guidance, the boys install all the footings measured to fit the steel building frame donated by a contractor in Ellsworth. The steel frame for the building is put together by the boys who use a combination of advice from experts and their own ingenuity. There is no crane available to lift the heavy steel into place, but the boys cut down trees to make thirty-foot logs and create three tripods that can be used to raise the beams after they are fastened together.

After the steel skeletal structure is bolted together the stonework begins. Progress is slow because the slabs of granite need to be cut to fit. The boys are supervised by Frank Manning, an adult volunteer who had been trained in granite masonry. With eyes protected by safety goggles, boys measure out each block to approximately eight inches wide and deep and twenty-four inches long. Once marked, the blue flame from an ultra-hot acetylene torch is drawn slowly along the cut lines and then the unneeded pieces are broken off with a hammer and cold chisel. Slowly, the facade of the building is taking shape.

To construct the granite walls, wooden forms are placed between the steel uprights fastened one-foot apart. The forms guide and hold the granite blocks in place while they are laid row upon row against the outside form, assuring straight lines of granite on the wall.

The boys accomplish all their goals that summer except for that one. Finishing the chapel building takes three more summers. Finally in 1979, three years after the first stone was harvested, Doc's dream is nearly realized with the walls and roof of the chapel building finished. The stone flooring, two large double front doors, and the window glass are not yet completed but the framework is ready for those final steps. Doc assigns Binocs, now an adult volunteer and advisor in his thirties known by his real name Phil, to supervise the building's completion. The boys are on the verge of celebrating another major accomplishment. An event later that summer would make the finishing of that building even more compelling.

Chapter Sixteen
The Legacy

Anne and Wick are walking quickly on the path from their cabin. The winds have picked up as darkness is approaching.

"They say the storm's a big one and coming in quickly," says Wick.

"How many boys are in Milbridge?" asks Anne.

"Just four," replies Wick. "They're on a garbage run to the In-Town House and will bring back the laundry."

"It's not like Doc to disappear like this," worries Anne.

"Yeah," says Wick, "he said he was going to check the other cabins. Now I'm concerned about the boys who are looking for him."

Anne and Wick arrive at the infirmary where Walt and Louise have been trying to use the camp's CB radio.

"Do the boys know that the storm's coming in?" asks Wick.

"They're all set for the worst," replies Walt. "But we're still looking for Doc."

Walt calls on the radio frequency they all normally use.

"Hello, In-Town House. Do you read me?"

There is nothing but static.

"Did you try Glenn's frequency?" asks Wick.

Walt toggles the radio to a different preset.

"Hello, Glenn. This is Walt at Camp Dyer Infirmary. Do you read?"

There is nothing but static on the radio again.

"Somehow this storm is affecting all our communications," says Walt.

The Boston Whaler arrives with the boys who are now unloading garbage bags filled with folded, clean laundry. It's very windy as the waves swell up moving the boat violently up and down. A tree branch snaps with a loud crack not far away. And then another.

In another slip, two boys stop working on the engine aboard the old police boat as the swell of the waves make their task more difficult. One of the boys on the Whaler calls out.

"You got her fixed yet?"

"Nah. She's gonna need some parts," says one of the boys. "We're calling it a day."

"It's gonna be a bad storm," says the boy on the Whaler. "Help us. Carry the laundry over to the lodge."

The two boys working on the police boat get out and pick up some of the bags along with the Whaler crew and head up the gangplank, which is moving up and down with the waves. A knot around one of the moorings anchoring the Whaler is slowly pulling loose, inch by inch.

The boat crew boys arrive at the lodge and go to the infirmary carrying the bags. Wick sticks his head out the door to greet the boys.

"Glad you made it okay. We were concerned with the storm coming in."

"Whalers are unsinkable," replies one of the boys.

"Did you tie her up good?" Wick asks.

"Yes sir," replies the boy. "We're fine and everybody's back. But the water's really kickin' up and the police boat can't be fixed because it needs parts."

"We can deal with that later," replies Wick. "We still can't find Doc."

On a path in the woods beyond Harry's Cabin, a tree has fallen in the high winds. Doc is lying on the ground next to it, showing no signs of movement. Sammy finds Doc under a large branch which apparently knocked him unconscious.

"Doc," shouts Sammy, "are you alright?"

There is another loud crash as the heavy wind takes down a nearby tree and now traps Sammy's legs. That crash wakes up Doc. He grabs the branch above him and slowly pulls himself up. After looking around, he sees Sammy trapped under the nearby tree.

"Can you hear me?" Doc shouts. "Are you okay?"

"I'm okay but I'm pinned down and can't move," replies Sammy. "Both legs are stuck."

Doc, who does not appear injured except for a big bump on his head, struggles to get to Sammy and now recognizes him.

"Hang on Sammy," shouts Doc. "I'm going to get you free."

Doc searches for something to use as leverage. He finds a large loose limb and is wedging it under the fallen tree branch like a lever to lift it up off Sammy's legs. He groans as he pushes but that doesn't work. Doc's breathing is difficult. He now finds a log and places it under his lever. He manages to put enough weight down on it to lift the branch that traps Sammy just enough to free his legs.

"I'm free!" Sammy shouts.

Doc collapses as the big branch comes back down. The wind is continuing to whip through the trees, and it is now dark and raining. Sammy gets up and is able to walk over to Doc on the ground.

"Doc!" he shouts. "You saved me. Are you okay?

Doc is mumbling so Sammy comes closer.

"Sammy, I'm having difficulty breathing. Can you walk? Can you make it to the infirmary?"

"Yes, Doc," says Sammy. "I'll bring back help."

As a boy from the boat crew is leaving the infirmary, lights are flickering. Sammy arrives with another boy. One of Sammy's legs is bloody. As Wick greets them at the door, Sammy is in a hurry to get the words out.

"I found Doc! He was knocked out by a branch that fell and then I was trapped by another tree. But Doc managed to free me when he woke up. He saved me! But now he's in trouble and needs help!"

"Is he conscious?" asks Wick with great urgency.

"Yes. I was talking to him. But he's not right."

"Where is he?" asks Wick.

"On the path on the other side of Harry's Cabin."

Walt has already pulled out a stretcher and is rushing out with two other boys as Wick follows behind while the rain and wind continue to menace. They reach Doc, place him on the stretcher, and carry him through the woodland path and out of the darkness into the light of the infirmary. Wick goes to work examining Doc while Louise treats Sammy's leg.

"How are you doing, Doc?" asks Wick. "Do you think anything's broken?"

Doc's voice is weak.

"I was knocked out and fell. But that's not … I think it's my heart."

Wick is listening to Doc's heart with a stethoscope and taking his pulse, then his blood pressure. Then he gives him a pill with a sip of water.

"This is aspirin," says Wick.

Anne whispers into Wick's ear. "His color is not good."

Wick whispers back into Anne's ear. "Beat's very irregular and weak. Pressure is critical. Can't do what we need to here. We've got to get him to Ellsworth."

Wick calls over to Walt. "Get the boat crew. We're taking Doc to Ellsworth."

"In this storm?" asks Walt.

"The Whaler can handle it and it's critical we get Doc to the ER."

Wick now speaks calmly to Doc. "You're going to be okay, Doc. We're getting you over to Ellsworth General."

"Good," replies Doc weakly. "Take good care of the boys, Wick. Promise me. The boys."

"Of course," replies Wick. "Right now, we're taking care of you."

A frantic boy from the boat crew rushes in and is out of breath. "The Whaler! The Whaler is gone! It got loose."

"Can you see it?" asks Wick.

"No, it's not in sight and it's hard to see in the dark and the rain."

"Then don't try to find it," replies Wick. "It's too dangerous."

Wick goes to the radio. "Glenn. Hello. Glenn. Can you read me? This is Wick on the island. We have an emergency."

There is nothing but static. Then, the power goes out. Flashlights are quickly turned on and Wick spots the flare gun hanging on the wall.

"Walt, take the flare gun. Send up a couple of flares. It's our best hope!"

Walt grabs the gun with a couple of flares and puts on his rain gear. He heads outside with a flashlight to face the wind and rain. As he gets close to the pier, Walt shoots off a flare toward the mainland that lights up the night sky. And then another, which also illuminates the wind whipped waves. There is a constant sound of tree branches breaking and a menacing clang clang from the channel marker in the bay.

Inside the infirmary, Sammy is now lying down with a bandage on his lower leg. Kerosene lamps light the room as Anne approaches Wick, who is attending to Doc.

"How's he doing?" she asks.

"He's comfortable. But his pulse is very weak."

At the pier, as Walt battles the wind and surveys the bay looking toward the mainland, there is a faint light which grows brighter. It's a powerful searchlight cutting through the stormy darkness. Glenn saw the flares and is now in his lobster boat along with Glenn Jr. The waves are rough as Glenn's boat approaches the dock.

"Doc needs to be taken to Ellsworth Hospital!" Walt shouts fantically.

Glenn Jr. jumps onto the landing but is having a difficult time securing the lines to the moorings as the boat and the floating dock are violently heaving up and down. Walt runs back to the infirmary. Moments later, two men, including Perky, the camp director, and two boys carry Doc on a stretcher through the rain, accompanied by Walt, Wick, and Anne following from behind. It's a balancing act as Doc is brought down the gangplank to the boat. Anne slips and Wick grabs her hand. Finally, with all aboard except the four who carried the stretcher, Glenn's boat once again cuts through the waves over towards Wyman's Landing where an ambulance is being summoned.

At Ellsworth General Hospital, Anne, Walt, and Glenn anxiously wait behind a large glass window with a view into an operating room where Doc is being attended to. The three are directed to a small, private waiting room. A half hour later, an emergency room cardiologist accompanied by Wick, both in scrubs, enter with grim faces. Words are useless as Wick puts his hand on Anne's shoulder and they embrace. Walt joins the tearful embrace as Glenn and his son look on.

The next morning, the storm is gone. When news of Doc's death reaches Louise on the island radio in the infirmary before dawn, she immediately heads over to the cabin occupied by Alan Frank, the current camp director.

"I feared as much," says Allie, as he is called. "He told me before we carried him down to the boat he wasn't going to make it, that the only thing keeping him alive was his pacemaker. He seemed angry at himself for being in that situation."

Allie quickly summons Fred, Southy, Phil, and boy director Johnny Krause to discuss how to break the news to the boys and what to do next. Somehow, the news has already gotten out and the boys are already assembling in the mess hall well before dawn. As the sun is rising, Johnny raises the island flag outside the mess hall to half-staff. Allie, Fred, Southy, Phil, Louise, and Johnny enter the mess hall wearing grim faces. Hugs are shared. Soon they are joined by Wick, Anne, and Walt who have been up all night and just arrived from Milbridge. As the smell of bacon fills the air from the kitchen, Wick gets up to speak.

"We lost Doc last night, despite the best efforts of Glenn and his son getting us across the bay in that storm. We located the Whaler and brought her back, thanks to Glenn. Most of you know that Doc had had a history of heart trouble. Last night was his third heart attack and while we got him to the hospital in time, he could not be saved. I know you all love Doc just as much as we do. And I call on you to honor Doc by fulfilling his last wish. He will be buried in one of the crypts in the chapel that you were so devoted to building."

Johnny raises his hand and speaks. "It's not ready. We have to finish it first."

"That you will," says Wick, "and we have confidence the job can be done. Doc's funeral will be held here in the chapel on August 10th. That's fourteen days from today."

Walt gets up to speak. "My father assures me that we will be spared no resource, so that we can complete this task. We will stay here after breakfast to organize the crews. Allie will coordinate all the efforts."

The building is still far from complete. While two crypts had been dug within the granite foundation below the floor, work on laying the actual floor had not been started. Two sets of double doors had not even been constructed yet, and none of the three huge cathedral windows and eight side windows had been put in place. Logic would have it that it would take more than a month to complete the task. But this was the Camp Dyer community where boys have become believers in overcoming the odds. For many of these boys, Doc had become a second father and he deserved no less than one-hundred-ten percent of their efforts. Word of Doc's passing spread on the mainland and among Camp Dyer alums. In a day's time eight of them, all fully grown adults and some of them members of the building trades, are enlisted to supervise and help the boys finish the building.

Before the woodwork along the walls can be completed all of the cracks in the granite subfloor have to be filled in with sand to ensure an even foundation for flooring stones. Dozens of yards of fine sand are brought in by barge from Milbridge. Boys transfer the sand shovel by shovel to a trailer pulled by a tractor to be brought to the work site. Once sand fills the entire floor space it must settle into the crevices. There is no tamping machine so the boys come up with an idea that involves bringing saltwater from the bay to pour over the floor to settle the sand while more sand is applied, over and over again, until the floor is solid and the tiles will not sink or become crooked. A steady stream of boys form a chain brigade to bring the sand and buckets of water to the site. Next, twelve hundred four-inch-thick one-foot square cement floor tiles, dyed red and manufactured earlier by the boys, are laid onto the floor.

While this progresses, a crew of boys and their supervisors install the three cathedral windows which have been painstakingly cut in the shape of an arch at the top. They also install eight side windows.

While this is going on, a carpentry crew is building two sets of heavy wooden double doors thirty-nine inches wide and ninety-six inches tall for the two entryways. To make the doors, oak planks are put together with wooden pegs in vertical fashion and cut to form an arch at the top when placed together. There are a series of holes drilled horizontally through the planks so they can be secured together with steel rods tightened at the ends with sunken bolts. Finally, the doors are stained brown with Val Oil, a high-quality varnish for exteriors designed to withstand harsh weather. This takes several coats over several days. The doors are hung on the building with heavy-duty hinges in the style of what one would see on a cathedral.

On day ten, the boys are still not finished. They must create a stone walkway leading from the wide path used as a roadway to bring materials. They must also build steps to lead up to the double doors. Finally, all the construction debris must be removed and carted away to prepare for Doc's funeral.

On day fourteen following Doc's death, it is sunny and calm on Narraguagus Bay. Anne, Wick, Walt, and Mary Anne are sitting by Doc's casket placed on the back of Glenn's boat, which is moving very slowly through the water toward Dyer Island. Also with them is Harry, now forty-six and still using a cane. Roseanne and Thelma are by his side.

"This is what Doc wanted," offers Anne to break the silence.

"A very special person," adds Harry. "He saved my life when I had the chainsaw accident. But there was so much more after that. He cared deeply about all of us and mentored us at our most needy times."

"He was a great friend, not just to me but to the boys and everyone he came in contact with," says Wick, his voice breaking with emotion. "He was truly an ambassador for mankind, not only here in Maine, but also in Boston and everywhere he went."

Gentle clangs from the bell on the nautical channel marker in the bay sound more like chimes as it rocks in the gentle water.

"There's a saying about people who die," continues Wick. "There is the death, and there is the second death when people forget you. Doc insisted he stay on the island after his death, and I don't think for Doc there will be any second death. I think his memory alone will go a long way in continuing to inspire the island boys."

Glenn's boat approaches the Dyer Island pier.

"Well look at that!" exclaims Wick.

There are perhaps hundreds of people lined up on and around the pier to greet Doc's body—solemn faces of campers, former campers, volunteers, and their families, and the older ones including Southy, Julio, and Jerry, joined by his father, judge Wysinger. Many others including dignitaries and businessmen and women who are highly regarded in the town of Milbridge and Washington Township are also there. There is Mr. Finney, owner of the town's gas station who often helped repair the vehicles on the island; Mr. Stout, owner of the local hardware store; and the local doctor who had attended to injuries the boys encountered when Wick and Doc were not present.

Horns sound from out in the bay. As Wick and the others aboard Glenn's boat turn around to look past Doc's casket they see dozens of boats sailing side by side in formation behind them sounding their horns.

The last stop on older Harry's walk with Wick and Johnny is the chapel building, the storied structure that now holds the heart and soul of the island. Inside, Harry, Wick and Johnny look at the engraved marker on the crypt where Doc is buried. There is also a plaque engraved in brass written by the Dyer boys at the time of Doc's death.

"Doc's legacy continues," they wrote, "to take form in boys' lives transformed, in troubled boys finding themselves, and in doing so, giving back, helping others on their way, in boys pursuing education and career paths they earlier never dreamed possible."

"When Doc died," Harry says to Johnny, "this chapel the boys worked so hard to build took on an even more important meaning. It then became and will forever be the Camp Dyer Memorial Building where Doc is laid to rest."

"I wish I could have known him," admits Johnny as he thinks about how he might play a role going forward. "So all the guys who came to camp and did this great stuff were really just like me?"

"That's right, Johnny," answers Harry.

Johnny looks directly at Wick. "Do you think they'll give me another chance?"

"There's only one way to find out," replies Wick.

"I'd like to go back and join the work on the pier," says Johnny. "I wanna be part of it."

He then turns to Harry. "Thank you, Dr. Thompson, for explaining all of this to me."

"Think nothing of it, Johnny," says Harry.

The sound of clangs from the channel marker is heard in the distance, but they now resemble church bells tolling.

"By the way," adds Harry, who realizes Johnny still does not connect him to his younger self, "you can just call me Harry."

"Harry?" replies Johnny with a look of astonished realization.

"That's right, Johnny. And if I can do it, you can also be a success. And you don't have to break the rules to get there."

In his mind, Johnny visualizes Harry on the roof with his pigeons, cutting his first tree, hanging roofing shingles with Jerry, being thrown in the water as first boy director, and getting his first college degree.

Minutes later at the pier work site, Johnny runs to the spot where stones are still being loaded into the framework and joins the relay. He is not rejected and is allowed to join the team.

Observing nearby, Mark, the senior counselor, looks at Wick.

"What's gotten into Johnny?" he asks.

"Beats me," says Wick as he displays a sneaky smile.

THE END

Postscript

The story of The Dyer Island Boys is based on real events beginning in 1946 brought about by the late Drs. Meredith Berry (Doc), Walter A. Wichern Jr. (Wick), and Anne Davis Wichern (Anne). Their dedication to service and the plight of inner-city teen boys led to the creation of The Berwick Boys Foundation (www.berwick.org). The Foundation continues to this day running year-round programs and the camp on Dyer Island, teaching teen boys about work, camaraderie, and the importance of community relationships. The three doctors' memories are preserved in the ongoing work of The Berwick Boys Foundation based in West Bridgewater, Massachusetts.

Author's Note

T he seed for this story was sprouted in the late 80s when my soon-to-be wife, Marina, and I visited Dyer Island at the invitation of her mother who was a nurse during the summers at Camp Berwick, a camp for teen boys run by the Berwick Boys' Foundation. I was impressed with the fact that the boys seemed to run the camp. I had jokingly referred to it as a real-life "Lord of the Flies" experiment.

During subsequent visits I later realized there was something profoundly important going on at the camp. In 1998, we brought our young children, Elena who was four, and Justin who was seven, for a week-long visit. I also brought with me a professional Canon XL-1 video camera, conducted a series of interviews, and shot candid scenes of camp activities in the hopes of fashioning a documentary. The interviews were transcribed, and I began to write about the camp. The documentary was never produced but I had decided I would write a screenplay about a fictional camp on that same island.

Since my story spanned from 1946 until 1996 it would require research into what life was like in the 1940s. Some of my fictional characters were based on real people I had interviewed and required additional research to build a world where my story would take place.

Later, some former "Berwick boys" shared with me their memoirs about the impact the camp had on them, one going as far back as 1949.

The Dyer Island Boys, which started as a screenplay, became an on-again, off-again project outside my main job as a network news writer. The first draft of the screenplay was completed in 2007 but with coverage notes I realized it needed to be re-written. Then, in the middle of the second draft, came a family tragedy. Our son Justin who was then seventeen died from an accidental drug overdose.

Our lives were turned upside down and the screenplay was put aside. We created a non-profit company, The Justin Veatch Fund, to award music scholarships in honor of Justin who had become a promising musician, on the verge of completing an album of his original music. We also decided we would "go public" about what happened to Justin in hopes we could prevent such a tragedy from happening to other young people. I developed a multimedia talk, *A Message from Justin*, that would eventually be presented to thousands of students in New York, New Jersey, and Connecticut schools. I also created the podcast, *The Drug Crisis: Faces Behind the Struggle*.

In 2016, the short documentary film *Whispering Spirits*, directed and produced by Sean Gallagher who had graduated earlier from the same school that Justin attended, told our story. The film premiered at Jacob Burns Film Center in Pleasantville, New York following a pattern of drug overdose deaths in our county. Discussion guides were developed for the film to teach parents and students that no family is immune from the perils of substance abuse.

Late in 2019, I picked up the screenplay again and was convinced *The Dyer Island Boys* was a story so compelling it needed to be finished. In its fifth draft, the screenplay advanced to the second round of the Austin Film Festival screenwriting competition. At that point, I realized it needed more work to gain the interest of potential producers and decided to temporarily shelve the screenplay and develop the story into a novel. The book, I reasoned, would require me to further develop the characters and create an even more complete and compelling story for readers. I believe it has, and I hope you agree.

Afterwards
Memoir of a "Berwick Boy"
by Phil Stewart

O n Dyer Island, it is a sunny yet cool early July morning in the year 2022. This summer marks my 69th year as a Berwick Boy, essentially my entire life since I first came to Camp Berwick at just 15. While Jeffrey's account begins at its early origins, mine began with its fifth season in 1953. It is I, then called "binocs," who during my first trip, in April of that year, weary after three intense days of real work, took the easy, but improper way out near the end by planting Christmas tree seedlings in bunches rather than individually.

What led me from this inauspicious beginning to winning the "most industrious," or "hardest worker" award at the concluding banquet was not a wise former Berwick Boy as in the story. Rather it began with the older boys, the boys who praised me when I did something right, who taught me the right way when I was uncertain, who corrected and supported me in a brotherly way. Then it was Doc Berry, the "Doc" of the story. "How are you feeling?" "How are you doing today?" "Tell me about it." With a comforting, accepting smile this is how Doc greeted us each morning. Unlike with my parents, I could talk to him and he would actually listen. He cared about me and every other boy at camp. He always encouraged us to be our best today, to have high dreams for tomorrow and the "guts," the courage to pursue them with all of our ability and passion. Then there was the work. Even as a five-year old, I remember constantly seeking to learn how things like houses, boats, or even simply window screens were made. At Berwick, not only did I have the chance to learn, but the responsibility to work with and teach others while we actually built log cabins! Fortunately, we had the main Lodge as a model for our work, but every day there were challenges we just had to figure out for ourselves. What a thrill! At fifteen, I was given the privilege of assuming grown-up responsibilities.

What makes all of this truly exceptional for me and for many Berwick Boys is the genuine majesty of Dyer Island itself. As I sit on my cabin's porch nestled just above the twenty foot high granite ledges lining our Northwest cove, I am calmed by the gentle lapping of the incoming tide, the sweet songs of birds sitting in the thirty-to-forty-foot fir trees lining our shores. It is the joy of walking along fir-lined, gravel roads built through years of hard work by Berwick Boys. It is the shared pleasure of sharing nutritious meals prepared by experienced Berwick Boys, now in their early twenties. As many boys, even first-year boys, have remarked to me over the years, being separated from the "real world" by two miles of water, living in this place of beauty, they somehow feel a new kind of freedom, a kind of paradise, a place that really feels like home, like a genuine community where they can find themselves through learning from and growing together with other boys.

A few real stories illustrate why Camp Berwick is a very special kind of community, a community created and sustained now for nearly seventy-five years by boys, of course under the leadership of Dr. Berry and the entire Wichern family – Drs. Walter and Anne and Adam, and Logan. "As I stepped on this island for the very first time, somehow the tensions, the fears that burdened me every day at home disappeared. For the first time in my life, I felt a kind of freedom," a 13-year-old boy reported to me some years ago. This was a troubled boy. He was an habitual liar and yet now he felt he had made real progress in overcoming it. I asked what happened. He responded, "I had a long talks over many evenings with the senior leader of our cabin. He helped me understand not only that lying to others was wrong, but it also made developing friendships very difficult." But then came the real insight. "Finally, I came to realize that if I am to stop lying to others, I first have to stop lying to myself!"

Alex, not his real name, first came to the island when thirteen years old. He had very intelligent eyes, was very articulate, seemed like a very nice young man, yet he often erupted in anger, at times uncontrollable. I wanted to understand why. My own experience working on conflict resolution around the Russian periphery, in Israel and Libya, and in US colleges and universities had led me to the feeling that encouraging people to talk while listening with caring and the intent to understand can help people better deal with their demons. Alex talked freely and openly. He had been conceived as a result of a casual relationship and never knew his father. While loving and caring, his single mother was a heroin addict who overdosed when he was only six. Fortunately, his loving and caring grandmother had raised him. But his anger was not only about that history. It also arose from the tensions he felt at not being "like" those other kids, with two parents, with family vacations and good schools.

Alex is now twenty-two and has spent more than half of the intervening nine summers at Berwick. Just recently, in response to my question, what has Berwick done for you, he responded that here, at Camp Berwick, although we do come from the most diverse backgrounds, "no one cares about that. We are all members of one community. We all work together, support and help each other. Berwick is the only place I really feel truly comfortable, truly at home."

The current Camp Director, now twenty-five and a Berwick Boy for fourteen years, told me that growing up his family moved around a great deal. Family life was not terribly healthy. It is the Berwick community that provides him with a feeling of "home," a place of friendship, caring, work and responsibility.

Now in my 84th year, I'm back at Berwick for the season. This is the thirty-fifth summer that I've spent at Berwick. As a college professor for twenty-six years, I was able to spend many summers here. In fact, entering my second year of graduate school, I married my sweetheart and brought her to Berwick for the summer. We enjoyed our honeymoon in my just completed cabin, a cabin with electricity when the generator runs, but no running water or bathroom – for those we used the lodge. After achieving tenure at the university, in 1973 with our two young children we began what would become a stretch of seventeen summers at Berwick, where our daughter eventually became a sailing instructor and our son boy director for two years. After a dozen years as a manager for Eastern Europe and the former Soviet Union for the Kellogg cereal company, I returned to Berwick in 2008 and have spent most summers since at camp.

The answer to why is both simple and complex. The simple answer, I believe, is that Berwick, what it stands for, what it has done and continues to do for me, is a fundamental part of my identity. Why this came to be so is the complex part. Doc Berry was my friend and primary life-mentor from 1953 until his passing in 1979. As a mentee, I wanted to be like him. He was a physician and surgeon, so I entered college with that same goal. A Berwick scholarship was a real help. I did fairly well in pre-med, but for some reason I still cannot fully explain, by the beginning of my junior year, I knew I had to become a political scientist with a focus on the Soviet Union.

In December 1972, Doc called and asked that I visit him. Once there, he explained that he had been given both a metal building and a large stock of raw-cut pink granite to create the memorial building of which we had talked back in 1961. Unfortunately, there was insufficient granite to cover the entire building. Could I design a building 30'x40' out of these materials and within these limits? Doc asked, which meant I could not and never would refuse. That very night I created a design incorporating three large cathedral windows, the central window six foot wide and eighteen feet high with arched tops.

Doc liked the design and said, "Of course you'll come up and help us turn this design into reality."

Admiration for Doc and love of building, especially such a beautiful but demanding building, doubtless formed my main motivations at the time. Thus began 7 summers supervising the construction of this building, together with Frank Cushing, a grown Berwick Boy with high level stone construction skills, and several entire generations of Berwick Boys. Doc Berry's funeral was held in the just completed Memorial Building on August 10, 1979.

During this period a subtle yet critical addition to my motivations developed. Working with teen-aged boys can be frustrating, as any teacher or parent knows. Given the changes occurring in our broader culture that undermined most authority structures and societal norms in the 1970s and 1980s, this was only more challenging. And yet, as the genuine smiles arise on each boy's face as, for the first time, he successfully hand cuts a curved piece of glass, or completes an entire eitheen foot wooden window frame, or successfully installs a row of granite, or uses an acetylene torch to give shape and form to raw granite, I experienced an ever-growing sense of pleasure, of satisfaction, of a sense that I was actually helping these boys to find themselves, to become the kind of men they wished to be. College teaching was good, but Berwick was better. At Berwick I got to really know the boys; I was able in a real way to help them gain self-confidence and character.

It never grows old. That is why, pushing eighty-five, I volunteer at Berwick. I am a Berwick Boy.

Philip D. Stewart Ph.D.

Senior Associate
Kettering Foundation
Secretary and Founding Board Member,
Sustained Dialogue Institute

Acknowledgements

I owe a debt of gratitude to the late Drs. Walter A. Wichern Jr. and Anne Davis Wichern who spent a good deal of time with me in 1998 talking about the origins of the Berwick Boys Foundation, and to son W. Adam Wichern III and daughter A. Logan Wichern who also spent time adding more stories and explaining their roles going forward. I also appreciate the Wichern family's warm hospitality whenever my family and I visited the island.

A special thanks to Brian McSweeney who first attended the camp in the 1990s and is now program director for the Berwick Boys Foundation; to John H. Rimmler, who attended the camp in 1949 and 1950, and provided rich descriptions of what it was like in those early days on Dyer Island; and to Phillip Stewart who first attended the camp in 1953, remains an important volunteer to this day, and provided camp stories and a touching memoir of his life-long commitment to Berwick in this book.

I'd like to thank editor Auriane Desombre who helped me expand the stories and characters in The Dyer Island Boys screenplay to bring them into full-throated characters for the novel.

I'd also like to thank editor Jessica Powers for helping me put these ideas into proper book form and bringing me forward toward actual publication.

A special thank you to my daughter, Elena, who provided editorial advice and constant encouragement; and to my wife, Marina, for understanding my obsession with getting this story told. And, lastly, I'd like to express thanks to her mother, the late Anna Louise Giusti, who as a camp nurse, introduced me to the island world.

Back Story Information

On page 33, I talk about gangs. The gangs from the 1940s were different from some of the notorious gangs that evolved later in New York and Los Angeles. They didn't fight over drugs, drive-by shootings were rare, and gang wars were mostly fought over turf and girls. These gangs were comprised of teen boys who came from the same ethnic backgrounds reflected in their neighborhoods and provided post war, working-class youth with a means of generating honor and defending their masculinity.

On page 36, I talk about Lavenburg Youth Detention Center. Among the oddities written about Lavenburg, it was said to have housed the infamous Lee Harvey Oswald as a teen. Oswald was quiet, small in stature, and was left alone by the other boys even though he was an easy target for bullying. According to reports, he was freed largely from the normal routine and allowed to check out library books to read in his room. Oswald would later go down in history as the assassin of President John F. Kennedy.

On page 40, I talk about the islands of Maine. There are more than four thousand small islands off Maine's coast and only a few of them have bridges connecting them to the mainland. Island dwellers are confronted with often intense environmental events. Fogs are thicker and storms are stronger.

On page 108, I talk about pliofilm bags. These bags were an early forerunner to plastic bags of today that weren't developed for consumers until the 1960s.

On page 124, I talk about seine fisherman. Seine fishermen travel up and down the coast looking for catch opportunities. When they cast a net across a cove at high tide, they create a trap for any fish swimming out of the cove as low tide approaches. It is legal to cast these nets, as long as the tops of them are under water when high tide arrives. There is no love between seine fishermen and locals, including lobstermen, as seiners take away from the local catch. The word seine has its origins in the Old English segne which comes from the Latin word sagene or drag-net.

Photos

The early photos of Dyer Island and Berwick Boys Camp are courtesy of
Phil Stewart and The Berwick Boys Foundation.

Author Picking Blueberries with Son Justin at age 7

Author's Daughter Elena at Age 4

Boarding the Whaler from Dyer Island for the mainland

Dr. Walter Wichern with Nurse Louise (on the right)

Lobsterman Lynden Perry who inspired the character Glenn

Lynden giving a tour to families duirng banquet weekend

Nurse Louise carrying lumber for the infirmary

Nurse Louise with Wichern dog, Coco

Walking on a Dyer Island path

Walter and Anne Wichern's son, Adam

Author at Welcome to Milbridge Sign 2021

Berwick camp population in 1980s

Phil Stewart 1979

Dr. Meredith Berry 1968

Dr. Meredith Berry on dock 1960s

Dr. Meredith Berry in a small boat which preceded the Boston Whaler

Dr. Meredith Berry in Wyman's blueberry fields 1976

Dr. Wichern with his daughter Logan

Dr. Meredith Berry and Dr. Walter Wichern 1960s

About the Author

Jeffrey Veatch is a retired newswriter-producer from ABC News Radio who took part in award-winning reporting for nearly 40 years and won a Writers' Guild Award in 2007 for *World News This Week*.

In 2008, Jeffrey's life took a drastic turn when his 17-year-old son, Justin, died from an accidental drug overdose. Justin was a talented musician on the verge of recording an album of his original work at the time of his death. The Veatch family vowed to finish his album (Permagrin: The Music of Justin Veatch) and founded the non-profit Justin Veatch Fund (thejustinveatchfund.org), which awards music scholarships to graduating high school seniors. As of 2022, sixty-one scholarships had been awarded.

In 2012, Jeffrey created the multi-media talk *A Message from Justin* which tells Justin's story with the goal of changing the attitudes of teens on the dangers of drugs. His talk has been presented to thousands of students in several states.

In 2014, *Whispering Spirits* (whispering-spirits.com), premiered at The Jacob Burns Film Center in Pleasantville, NY. The film, along with its discussion guides, has been distributed to anti-drug coalitions, schools, and community organizations nationwide.

In 2018, Jeffrey created the podcast *The Drug Crisis: Faces Behind the Struggle* (facesbehindthstruggle.libsyn.com) which is on multiple media platforms.

He has served as a judge for The Writers' Guild of America Awards in radio division competitions.

In addition to writing *The Dyer Island Boys* novel and screenplay, Jeffrey loves to cook and is a former competitive runner who is now an avid cyclist. He lives with his wife, Marina, and their cats Cali and Gray in Yorktown Heights, New York.

www.ingramcontent.com/pod-product-compliance
Lightning Source LLC
Chambersburg PA
CBHW041747010726

47507CB00008B/314